The Sound of His Horn

Black Curtain Press
PO Box 632
Floyd VA 24091

ISBN 13: 978-1627553612

First Edition
10 9 8 7 6 5 4 3 2 1

The Sound of His Horn

Sarban

Forward
by Kingsley Amis

Forward
by Kingsley Amis

We can be pretty certain that our literary tastes are arrived at not so much by conscious choice as in response to the less-than-conscious demands of our temperament. Thus the reader of westerns isn't in the first place concerned with a particular stretch of American history, nor does he simply want a fast narrative with plenty of action. What he likes, I imagine, is hearing about a special kind of heroic society and a special, simplified code of morality and honor. The idea of gun law satisfies his nature in a way that tough ethics or private-eye ethics, for instance, can't. The same sort of process, with its different sets of results, is at work in the mind of the science-fiction addict and the fantasy addict.

The distinction between science fiction and fantasy has been thrashed out over and over again without anything very positive emerging. It will not quite do to say that science fiction tries to make its marvels plausible while fantasy doesn't bother with any of that To take only one example: the ghost stories of M. R. James work hard and successfully to convince the reader that there are circumstances in which a ghost can be expected to show up, to offer a chain of "logic" that will explain an apparition just as satisfactorily as time travel, etc, is explained by the "logic" of the science-fiction writer. And similar objections can be made against all other attempts to distinguish between the two modes—all that I have seen, at any rate. On the other hand, most of us usually know which of the two we are reading in any given case. The definitions may not fit properly but there are always plenty of clues.

Science fiction is likely to be interested in the future, whether near or remote. The bias of fantasy is correspondingly backward-looking, to the mythologies of demons and werewolves and mermaids. When it does portray the future, it does so typically in terms borrowed from the past, dressing everybody up in ceremonial robes and locating them in some kind of feudal or medieval world. Again, the horrors of science fiction, when not interplanetary, are always urban; its paradises, as in the work of Clifford D. Simak and others, are rural. But it is right there in the country that horrible things happen to characters in fantasy stories, to the terrified old couple cut off from humanity in Shirley Jackson's *The Summer People*, to the village at the mercy of an omnipotent three-year-old sadist in Jerome Bixby's *It's a Good Life*.

To take it a stage further back, one could argue that fantasy appeals to deeper and darker instincts than does science fiction. The fears that find expression in it are not rational fears of an overgrown technology or a gradually encroaching totalitarianism, but ancient irrational fears of that world which science has blotted out of conscious thought, the world of unseen forces beyond the extrication of science, to be seen most clearly in terms of the past, obviously, or in remote areas where the rule of science does not run. And so science fiction, the active, progressive agent, is hopeful about man's ability to improve himself via reason; fantasy, reactionary and pessimistic views man as the hopelessly corrupt plaything of blind, random influences. It is in this sort of way that we can explain the air of arbitrariness and cynicism, the slices of cruelty, disgust and despair, that are characteristic of so much fantasy writing, and here lies its appeal to our temperament. I hope I haven't sounded puritanical about this, by the way; I myself prefer science fiction to fantasy on the whole, and of course I think this is right; but the view of life I have ascribed to fantasy is one which has its attraction for most of us at certain times. Occasionally, too, a piece of fantasy comes along written with a skill and energy that make us revise our preconceptions.

The Sound of His Horn is such a piece. It certainly is fantasy in all sorts of ways, starting with the obvious point that the parallel universe in which the main story takes place is not to be approached by any kind of scientific technique, nor is its existence to be explained along any possible scientific lines. Alan Querdilion, retelling his experiences, feels he ought to be able to explain them away as a madman's dream, for this

would be the best proof of sanity—not by my own sanity alone, but the sanity of all this order that we believe in, the proper sequence of time, the laws of space and matter, the truth of all our physics; because you see, if I *wasn't* mad there must be a madness in the scheme of things too wide and wild for any man's courage to face.

To question the validity of "all this order that we believe in" is the typical starting-point of fantasy, and "a madness in the scheme of things" is its typical subject matter. When Querdilion awakes to find himself in a future world dominated by the Nazis after their victory in World War II (now renamed the War of German Rights), he is acting out a favorite maneuver of fantasy and indeed a nightmare that reaches a long way back into the past: the dreadful awakening into an environment that is human but changed. The character's response, and the reader's invited response, are shock and horror, expressed most powerfully in Kafka's *The Metamorphosis*, which inverts the usual procedure by changing the character (into a huge roach) and leaving the environment unchanged.

Sarban's achievement is not on the scale, but the shock and horror are genuine enough. They are given an added edge by the relative plausibility of the society in which Querdilion finds himself marooned. If the Nazis had in fact won their war, we could have expected to see—those of us who were still around—a systematic development of the master-race concept into a kind of feudal structure, with a small oligarchy of immensely powerful and capricious overlords, a middle stratum of fiendishly conscientious Party administrators, and a huge slave-proletariat absolutely subject to the whim of their masters, even to lengths of providing them, as here, with human game for the chase. No less plausible is the rural environment, which connects up with those distorted Nazi dreams of an older Germany inhabited by hard-riding, hard-drinking barons (Hermann Goering, cleverly invoked in the novel, is the example here) and bands of clean-limbed young Nordic foresters (compare the countrified elements in the activities and dress of Nazi youth organizations).

I said earlier that a rural setting was a settled ingredient of fantasy, but inspection reveals that Sarban uses it, and much else, in a way more characteristic of science fiction. The long prelude, again, with its cheerful fireside atmosphere, is aimed at setting up a reassuring basis of familiarity while preparing for a violently contrasting plunge into the unfamiliar. The average writer of fantasy does not go about things in this way. Even if he is interested in plausibility, he seldom goes beyond inducing us to suspend our disbelief for the duration of the story; Sarban remains plausible on reflection as well. Further, to present a whole society and way of life, not merely a situation, in relatively convincing terms is even less typical of fantasy. And just as *The Sound of His Horn* invites comparison with science fiction in its concern to present a coherent picture that borders on our own experience (plus a few bio-technological details about the breeding of slaves), so it stands as a challenge to science fiction in its originality.

The nightmare futures envisioned by writers like Frederik Pohl or Ray Bradbury are often brilliantly detailed and imaginative, but as noted they are always urban, metropolitan, technological, consumptional, managerial. Sarban's rural hell is just as clearly visualized, furnishing a critique of that huge tribe of authors who can only see future systems of oppression in terms of brainwashing and too much television, and acting as a timely reminder that a nonurban hell is not only imaginable, but possible. There is no reason to suppose that the currently accelerating dislike for megapolitan life will not eventually explode into action, and if that is in the cards we have Sarban to show us the falsity of the sentimental consensus—to be found outside science fiction as well as within it—that it is only the city and the machine and the ad which kill, that the country rehumanizes. One could add that it is a relief to meet a story of this general kind—the nasty Utopia—that doesn't adopt the hackneyed science-fiction solution of showing a band of the oppressed killing the local overlord and freeing his prisoners before marching off into the sunset to reconquer the world for democracy. I like that prospect all right, but it comes up rather more often than it need—and much more readily than it in fact would if any of these imagined hells, urban or rural, came halfway to reality. An occasional dose of pessimism, such as Sarban provides, is good for you.

With all this said, it remains true that *The Sound of His Horn* is a fantasy, not least in the extra sense that (as it would take a very unsophisticated reader not to see) the propelling force of the book, what gives it its irresistible energy and conviction, is a sexual "fantasy" uniting several features of abnormal psychology—I use the word *abnormal* in a purely descriptive, not emotive, sense. The whole notion of hunting with girls as the quarry; the use of savage dogs in the pursuit; the selective nudity of the girls' costumes; the details of the way they are trussed up before being handed over to their captors; the cat-women, similarly half-undressed but with taloned gloves on their hands, who tear living deer to pieces and eat them; the third set of girls lined up as living candle-bearing statues; all these things could be paralleled from many a couch-side notebook. Alan Querdilion watches and reports everything with horror and revulsion, but at length and in detail, and there is a lot to watch and report.

It is not difficult to see in what is described here a fascinated enjoyment of sadistic fancies, and in the attitude of the describer a hypocritical moral revolt inserted to enable author and reader to retain their self-respect while continuing to enjoy themselves. Some people, having got this far in analysis, may find it hard to go on reading the book with pleasure. I understand this reaction, but I do feel it simplifies things too much. There need be nothing hypocritical in Querdilion's attitude, for we are not to assume that sadism is incompatible with moral feeling (though I admit that the two don't actually go hand in hand). More important, much of the novel is taken up with Querdilion himself being hunted, and I can find no indication that he or Sarban are secretly getting some discreditable thrill out of that. To quote a parallel case, Bram Stoker may have had a private obsession which he expressed as vampirism in Dracula, but this suspicion doesn't make us feel that the terror experienced by Jonathan Harker and Dr. Seward, Dracula's opponents, is somehow not important, or forced, or unreal, nor is the book as a whole thereby rendered in any way suspect.

A less obvious, and perhaps less close, parallel is provided by some of the earlier poems of Keats, which can be read as autoerotic fantasies. In *The Eve of St. Agnes* we find, as well as straightforward sexual elements, a characteristic obsession with elaborate foods and drinks, with rich furnishings and apparel, with nobility and protocol, with the past, with physical danger, all of which reappears to an uncanny degree of exactitude in *The Sound of His Horn.* But to read the poem in this way, however interesting to the amateur psychologist, is to do it less than justice as a poem, and on its different level Sarban's work can claim the same kind of freedom from moral censure. Moreover, there is something to be said for the view that fantasy of this sort (like the western with its ruthlessness, its fights and shootings) can have a therapeutic value by enacting sexual and other "fantasies" at a safe remove from reality. Alternatively, the eventual fate of the girl Kit North, Querdilion's ally, furnishes a telling criticism of the original "fantasies" by demonstrating what they really amount to in terms of human irresponsibility and pain, by revealing Count von Hackelnberg, the sadistic master-huntsman, in all his brutishness. In any event, *The Sound of His Horn* strikes me as far less repugnant than many nonfantasy novels whose moral obliquities are less overt.

Perhaps I wouldn't have cared to go as far as this in my defense if I didn't believe so much in the literary qualities of the book. The gradually accelerating narrative, with its chain of horrors that close in on Querdilion with equal inevitability, is set out in a prose that falls occasionally into stiffness but much more often strikes the reader hard with its nervous intensity, its power of excited visualization in detail and its freshness. It is a style equally removed from the would-be poetical whimsicality of so many stories of fantasy and the flat anonymous woodenness or toughy banality of so much science fiction. The scene that remains most vividly in the memory is, appropriately, the final one at the electrified fence that borders the Count's domain— the dead girl, the hideous parody of a hunting party with its apparatus of cat-girls and dog-boys and bloodhounds, Hackelnberg himself with his (rightly) inexplicable sparing of Querdilion and mysterious final utterance, above all the play of moonlight and shadow, the shimmering of the lethal fence and the blinding beams of the watchtower searchlights. If Orson Welles can get onto a horse I know whom I would choose to film all this.

The Sound of His Horn has its aural effects too, not less haunting. The first intimation of what may be in store for Alan Querdilion is the sounds he hears at night in his warm hospital bed: "they were notes of a horn, sounded at long intervals, each one as lonely in the pitch dark and utter silence, as one single sail on a wide sea." From then on this eerie and impressive image, encountered by day or night, near or far, never recurs without bringing a chill. In its archaic associations, its evocation of pageantry, its reminder of the hunter's carefree gusto together with the terror of the hunted, it sums up the whole content and atmosphere of this novel, this strange combination of daydream and nightmare. So compelling is it that I shall always feel a slight twinge whenever I am reminded of the innocent English hunting song from which the title is taken.

1

"It's the terror that's unspeakable."

We all looked at Alan Querdilion. It was the first time he had spoken in the argument; almost the first time he had spoken since dinner. He had merely sat there smoking his pipe and looking from one speaker to the other with that look of mild wonder on his face which seemed to be habitual with him nowadays: a look that reminded me not so much of a child's innocence, as of the simpleness of a savage to whom the sound of your strange voice is a wonder distracting him from attention to the sense of what you are saying. After observing that look for three days I understood what his mother meant when she had said privately and sadly to me that the Germans had not released all of Alan from prison in 1945.

I had not seen Alan for nearly ten years, since the day in 1939 when he went off to join his ship as a lieutenant of the R.N.V.R. Perhaps one assumes too readily that time and a bitter war are great changers of character: later, I was astonished that I had been so little troubled to mark the change in Alan. Even that transformation from the buoyant, self-confident, gay young man of abounding energy, of such prowess in all sports, to this silent, inactive and wondering creature, had been but a part of the general flatness and fading of the world and the subduing of strength and spirits that England seemed to have suffered since 1939. It was easy to forget that Alan had not been like that before.

It was easy for the first three days of my visit to Thorsway—until Alan's mother spoke to me. Then, by very quietly and sadly asking me what was wrong with Alan, she forced me to recognise the change in him. It was as if she thought that I who had been his closest friend all through his school and university days would hold the key, or could pay the ransom of that part of his mind which was still held captive somewhere. That was how she put it: "They" had sent back his body, more or less sound, and so much of his wits as would carry him through the daily business of managing the small farm his father had left him, but they had kept the rest behind. What had they done to him? Or what had he done to himself during his four years in a prisoner of war camp?

I tried uncomfortably to evade the role of amateur psychiatrist that this confidence seemed to invite me to assume. I uttered some generalisations about war experience and the monotony of prison life—such commonplaces as my memories of conversations with a good number of other former prisoners of war suggested to me; and, besides, I added, perhaps unkindly, Alan was ten years older; she could not expect the boy in him to live for ever. She shook her head. "It's something more personal than that, and I'm sad mainly for Elizabeth's sake." I could but try to assure her half-heartedly that I did not notice so great a change in him.

Certainly the other people there in the drawing-room that particular winter evening seemed to take Alan's inaction or absence of mind for granted, and they had known him well before the war. I think they had no more expected him to intervene in the argument than I had.

There were the Hedleys and their daughter, Elizabeth. Major Hedley was an old neighbour of the Querdilions, retired now, and farming in Thorsway, like Alan. There was also Frank Rowan, Alan's cousin, who was a lecturer in economics at a northern university. Like myself he was spending a week of his vacation with them. These two had known Alan since he was a child. If they thought something was wrong with him they never breathed a word of it to me: they seemed to treat him as a simple, good-natured fellow, just the chap to make a reluctant tractor go or tinker with an ailing oil-engine, one who might astonish you by the agility with which he would shin up on to a barn roof or vault a five-barred gate, but not a man you'd ever expect to contribute anything to such an argument as we had that evening after dinner.

Yet his mother was right. That argument more than anything else showed me the change in him. He was not a fox-hunter, but he liked fox-hunters and he loved all exercises of bodily strength and skill. In pre-war days he had always subscribed to the Saxby Hunt, in whose country Thorsway lay, and if he did not hunt with them it was because he had always been a runner rather than a rider. He had been a notable cross-country man at Cambridge; a very good all-round athlete, but no horseman. In his country setting I thought of him as the descendant of a line of yeomen rather than squires, one of that old race of Lincolnshire farmers whose delight was in greyhounds rather than foxhounds, who took their long-dogs coursing over the windy wolds on foot. But country sports were in his blood. Had Frank attacked fox-hunting in the old days as he did this evening Alan would have been the first to sail into action in defence of it.

But now he had kept silence for an hour and a half while the others went at it hammer and tongs: Frank Rowan, in truculent mood retrospectively fighting the lost battle of the anti-fox-hunting Bill only recently then defeated in the House of Commons, was witty, bitter, provocative and, to my mind, something less than polite to his hostess and her neighbours when he stressed the moral and intellectual insufficiency of those who practised or approved blood-sports. Major Hedley combined the modesty of a good professional soldier with a countryman's knowledge of hunting; he defended the cause on his own well-known ground and steadily refused to be lured into regions where Frank might take him at a disadvantage with his weapons of philosophy and psychology.

Not so Elizabeth Hedley. And that was the strangest of all, that Alan was not moved to make at least some murmurs of support for her, or sketch some gesture of rescuing her from the tangle of self-contradictions and inconsistencies into which Frank, with wicked dialectic, led her. Her ardour would have fired a man far less susceptible to the influence of spirited young women than Alan had been in the old days; now it seemed merely to bewilder him, or—as I felt once or twice—to alarm him.

Elizabeth was twenty-two, good-looking and lively. She had been born and brought up in Thorsway and had been a devoted admirer and companion of Alan's when she was a child of eleven or twelve before the war. Horses had been a passion with her all her life, and her conversation with me on the few occasions when I had met her during these three days in the village had been all of hunting, horse-shows, Pony Club meetings and the bringing up of foxhound puppies. She, if anyone, might have been expected to be distressed at the change in Alan. Yet, apparently, she had agreed to marry him soon after he came back from captivity, and no one but Mrs. Querdilion had given me the slightest hint that all was not well between them. There had not even been any suggestion of pity or protection in Elizabeth's behaviour towards Alan, as far as I could see: nothing of the solicitude such as a warm-hearted girl would have shown for him if he had come back from the wars crippled or blinded.

I say they were engaged, but I do not know that the engagement had ever been announced; I took it for granted from the way Major and Mrs. Hedley and Alan's mother spoke of the pair. It is true, I wondered a little why they were drawing out the engagement so long, though Elizabeth would have been only about eighteen when Alan came back, and no doubt her people preferred her to wait; but there seemed to me to be no reason why they should not have married during the last year.

Then, as I observed Elizabeth during the heat of this argument about fox-hunting, and saw the covert alarm in the gaze poor Alan turned on her as she retorted with brilliant indignation to Frank's attacks, I gave his mother credit for perceiving the truth. Alan had lost his spirit; his manhood was lost or sleeping; something had so altered him that the girl's animation, youth, ardour and beauty daunted him. He was simply afraid of her, and I could guess that though others might take their engagement for granted neither he nor she did, for he had not had the courage to ask her. His mother knew that he would lose her if he did not pull himself together, and I found myself sharing her anxiety. They would be such a good match; Elizabeth would provide just that quickening and re-animating that Alan seemed to need; I refused to believe that he was so fundamentally changed in nature to be indifferent to her physical beauty; all he needed was some old friend to make him aware of the risk he was running through letting this acquired diffidence get the better of his real desires.... Before the argument was at an end I had accepted the role Mrs. Querdilion had designed for me.

The argument ended very unexpectedly. Frank, I am sure, was keeping up his end more for the amusement of provoking Elizabeth than because he was seriously opposed to fox-hunting. Their exchanges, as I have suggested, became very brisk and, to my mind, all but insulting, though I suppose they knew each other well enough to be able to box each other's ears verbally without real offence. Still, after a certain time, Frank began to extricate himself and, little by little, turned the argument to banter and joking until it had reached the point where he could say:

"Well, after all, nobody's improved on Oscar Wilde's definition of fox-hunting: The unspeakable in pursuit of the uneatable."

Then Alan took the pipe out of his mouth and said in a quiet, matter-of-fact tone:

"It's the terror that's unspeakable/'

It was the apparent irrelevance of the observation and the abruptness of the transition to seriousness again that surprised us, as much as the fact of Alan's taking part in the argument at all. Frank and the Major looked blank, but Elizabeth, after an uncomprehending stare, said sharply, and with a just perceptible note of hostility in her voice:

"Terror? What terror?"

Alan leaned forward with his pipe clasped between his hands and frowned at the cat peacefully curled on the hearth-rug. He found it very difficult to say what he wanted, and we waited—we three men, at least, with a too obvious tolerance of his inarticulateness. The Major, amused now after his surprise, smiled encouragingly as one might to a child having difficulty with the beginning of a recitation.

"I mean," Alan said at last, still staring at the cat, "I mean it's the fear something feels when it's being hunted: that's what you can't describe; that's what's unspeakable. You can describe the people all right..."

Elizabeth had raised her brows and made her eyes very wide; her whole expression spoke of objection and challenge; I expected her to burst out with "Rubbish!" and assail him with the same vehement assertion she had fired off at Frank Rowan already a dozen times that evening; that a violent death is the natural end of all wild creatures, that it is the most merciful one, that animals have no imaginations to paint them the terrors of death before it comes—all the familiar contentions used by fox-hunters who are imprudent enough to defend their sport by attempting to put the fox in the witness-box. I was sure she was going to retort all that upon Alan, for the expressions of her face were as easy to read as a child's, but before the words had passed her lips her thoughts were quite evidently diverted suddenly into another and, it struck me, an entirely unfamiliar channel. The objection, the eagerness to retort disappeared from her face; she gazed steadily at Alan, whose attitude seemed to express a greater worry and uneasiness as he bent forward, averting his head from her, and I fancied I saw some such absorbed interest as might have been native to the cat between them come into her still round eyes. Impossible to tell then what discovery, what new interpretation of experience his words had opened to her. I could only guess that for her the subject of argument had suddenly changed from fox-hunting to Alan himself and that she divined that the fear he spoke of had in some strange way something to do with herself, and instinctively, with that new realisation she had become watchful, intent on maintaining the privacy of her thoughts. She waited for one of the others to speak.

But Mrs. Hedley was gathering herself together to depart. Alan got up and went silently out to put on the hall lights, and after we had seen the visitors off he took a lantern and went to see about some task in the yard.

Mrs. Querdilion said goodnight very soon, and Frank, after laughing and joking a little, pleased at his success in the argument and amused at Alan's odd intervention, took himself off to bed. Not having the habit of such early hours, I poured myself out some beer, turned off the lights in the sitting-room and drew the fire together.

The cat jumped onto the arm of my chair and, tucking its forepaws under its chest, settled down with me to stare at the glowing coals.

A footfall and a cold draught roused me, not from a doze, but from contemplation of a long succession of memories that followed each other through my mind as involuntarily as the images of a dream. Alan had come in again. I heard him quietly bolting the outer door. I got up to put on the light, but bumped into him at the sitting-room door. He gasped and seized me by the coat; then, as I spoke, he gave a short relieved kind of laugh, and relaxed his hold.

"I forgot the cat," he said. "Is she in here? I thought you'd all gone to bed."

His voice sounded unsteady. I put on the light and was shocked to see his face quite white from the start I had given him. Full of contrition, I apologised for lurking there in the dark. He muttered with obvious embarrassment that I should take no notice, and came over to the fireplace, making a show of looking about him for the cat, but moving nervously and jerkily, taking too long to recover from the start.

I thought it better to say something and struck straight into the evening's main topic:

"I shouldn't wonder if it's just dawned on Elizabeth tonight that there might be something in the humanitarian case against hunting. It was what you said, of course; or the way you said it. Made her look a bit thoughtful, it seemed to me." He turned on me sharply.

"She's hunted all her life. Why should anything I say make any difference?"

It was as clear as daylight to me then that he and she had argued this matter before—and with some heat. I could guess they had squabbled, and trivial as a difference of opinion on such a matter between two lovers might seem to me, I could see its importance to them, in a life where hunting was taken seriously. But why should Alan not want her to hunt now?

"Oh, I don't know," I replied. "I should have thought your opinion counted for something—a good deal more than Frank's, anyway. And there was a time when every word you uttered was an oracle to her."

He stooped and put another log on the fire, as if he had quite forgotten that he had been about to go to bed. Then he stood with bent shoulders for some time silently watching the log smoulder and smoke. At length, without looking at me, and in a controlled voice he said:

"My mother's been talking to you about me and Elizabeth, hasn't she?"

"Well..." I said. "About you.... She's a bit worried. Thinks you've got something on your mind, I believe. Personally I don't see any difference in you, except that you seem to lose your tongue at times, and, if you don't mind my saying so, your nerves aren't in any too good a state. I don't think you're very fit, and you ought to be in this farming life. It isn't the bottle, is it?"

He laughed. "I've been thinking these three days you've been here that we're just the same pair of blokes that we were before, really. Seeing you has been good for me. I know I haven't altered after all."

"Well," I said, "character and affections ought, no doubt, to remain constant, but there'd be little hope for man if experience didn't alter behaviour and opinions. You've had six years of war and imprisonment. I can well understand a man having different views about all sorts of things after that."

"Yes," he said. "You'd understand. Or at any rate, you'd be interested. Look here!" He straightened up abruptly and turned round. "You're not tired, are you? Mind if I tell you something? Let me fill your glass, then sit down and I'll tell you a tale."

He poured out some beer for us both and switched off the light, then stirred the fire till it broke into flame.

"I can tell it better like this, by firelight," he said as he settled himself in the armchair opposite me, "and if I bore you you can go quietly to sleep without my noticing it."

We filled our pipes and I waited.

"I've not told this to anybody," he began. "Not to my

mother, or Elizabeth. And before I tell it to you, I want to make the point that it is a tale: just a tale, you understand, that I'm telling you because I think it'll entertain you; I'm not asking you to listen so that you can tell me what my trouble is. I know that perfectly well myself, and there's nothing anybody can do about it It's just a question of waiting to see if it happens again. It hasn't recurred in three years; if I get through another year without it happening I shall take it that it won't happen again and I shall feel I can safely ask Elizabeth to marry me and all will be well. She can ride to hounds and I shan't quarrel with her over that —so long as she doesn't expect me to; and she won't."

2

'I am not mad, most noble Festus.' No. But I have been. Not just unbalanced, or queer, but beautifully barmy; certifiable beyond the shadow of a doubt. I'm all right again now. Really all right, I believe. Only, having slipped into the other gear very suddenly once, I know how easily and swiftly it can happen, and sometimes an unexpected thing frightens me for a moment— until I've made sure that I am still on this side of the wall, so to speak.

It's not unknown, of course, for a man in a prisoner-of-war camp to go round the bend. It can happen to anybody, and not necessarily to the highly strung ones, or the ones with most worries. I'd seen them before it happened to me. We called them happy. I think I know the reason for that peculiarly indifferent air they have: they just don't know what's going on in this world while they're so busy in the other. And you feel extraordinarily sane, you know. I am sure, in my own case at least, that I was twice as active in mind, twice as sensitive to what was going on while I was round the bend as I was after I came into the straight again and was back in the cage once more.

I was glad it was a different cage they put me back in. None of the fellows there knew that I had been off my head, and the psychiatrists passed me as perfectly normal when we all got out. Of course, I didn't tell 'em what I'm telling you.

We were dive-bombed and sunk off Crete in 1941, and I had two years in a camp in Eastern Germany: Oflag XXIX Z. Very familiar it all grew to me, that very little world: barbed wire, of course, jerry-built huts, too cold in winter, too hot in summer, the messy washing-places, the smelly latrines, the light sandy soil, the black pine-forest in the distance and the goons on the sentry-perches: all the little contrivances and tricks and studies and inventions that seemed so important to us—well, that *were* important when your world was reduced to such dimensions.

I flattered myself that I stood prison life a good deal better than most people. I'm never really unhappy anywhere if I can find something to do with my hands, and it's surprising what a busy artisan you can turn yourself into in such circumstances if you have a bent that way. I'm really proud of some of the things I made out of old tins. I kept my mind working objectively, too. I set out to re-learn my Greek. It would have been more sensible, perhaps, to learn German, but I suppose the Greek appealed to me because it seemed so clean and fresh and had nothing to do with the camp.

Well, I mention this just to indicate that I was a fairly cheerful prisoner. Of course, I missed getting my right amount of exercise, but, considering the low diet, I probably did well enough on the gymnastics we organised. Then, I had no particular family troubles. I got letters from my mother and Elizabeth as regularly as anyone got letters, and as long as those two were all right I had nothing more of that sort to worry about. True, you might say that the enforced company of one's own sex alone is a deprivation that might set up mental strains—but I don't know: it was the same for me as for everybody else; one thought of the pleasures of dalliance, of course, but I think it helps you to take the holiday from them more philosophically if you've had a normal fair share of those pleasures before you go into the bag. It seemed to trouble the boys most; not chaps of my age.

No, looking at it quite honestly and objectively—and a prison camp is a good place in which to measure deviations from the norm of behaviour—I would have said that I'd have been one of the last to go off my rocker.

But there it is. I did. Of course, it may have been the shock—the electric shock or whatever it was that I got: I'm coming to that. But there again, I'd had far worse shocks before. I'd been torpedoed twice in three months in the North Sea, not to mention the odd bomb. Those jolts shook my body far more than the shock I got at the fence at Hackelnberg, but they did not unhinge my mind.

Ah well! You'd not believe the times I've been over the evidence for my sanity during these two years, and the care with which I've sifted it to find the little flaw, the sign of hidden weakness, and I never can find it. I ought to; I ought to be able to find out why I went out of my mind for a period, because, don't you see, that would be the best proof of sanity—not my own sanity alone, but the sanity of all this order that we believe in, the proper sequence of time, the laws of space and matter, the truth of all our physics; because you see, if I wasn't mad there must be a madness in the scheme of things too wide and wild for any man's courage to face.

And it's ironical to remember that I was looked on as the steadiest, sanest, most reliable old horse in the whole camp. There was the Escape Committee—the best brains among the senior officers: they could judge a man better than most of your psychiatrists. They, with all their experience of crack-brained schemes, would have spotted my flaw if anyone could have done. On the contrary, I had a part, as adviser or assistant, in pretty well every attempt at escape that was made. I became a sort of consultant to planners, the chap whose expert advice was sought before a plan was put up to the Escape Committee for sanction.

Escape, of course, was the medium, as it were, in which all our thoughts existed; our little occupations and amusements were the surface waves of life and the study of escape the sea that buoyed up all we did.

In practice all escape plans were variations of one method. There was only one way of solving the basic problem of passing the wire. That was moling—tunnelling. I had a hand in the planning of many tunnels and was a member of many different combines for digging and hiding the earth; but there was not one successful escape from Oflag XXIX Z up to the time when my partner and I made our attempt.

I won't go into all the details of the planning and the digging. They'd prove just the opposite of what I'm trying to prove to you by this story, because that tunnel was exceedingly well planned and well dug. The whole camp backed us to succeed.

We did it on a night towards the end of May, an hour before moonrise. The exit of our tunnel was a hundred yards beyond the wire, leaving us a fifty-yard dash to a tongue of the pine-forest. The simplest application of the principles of tunnelling, we argued, was the likeliest to succeed. Most plans failed because the tunnel was not taken far enough beyond the wire. The labour was so heavy and the time so long that once you were under the wire the temptation to stop digging and risk the longer dash was too strong to be resisted. We resisted it, and succeeded at least so far as to gain the black concealment of that tongue of pine forest without the alarm being given. We had used the old cover of getting our confederates inside to start a fight in one of the blocks in order to distract the guards' attention: a very old trick, but it worked.

Then, we had resisted the temptation also to try to plan the next stages in detail. Both of us, Jim Long and I, had our own ideas of the best way to travel in Germany in war-time and we agreed to go our own way about it. Stettin was the place to make for: there we should make contact with someone in the underground escape organisation and get a Swedish ship. That was the broad outline, and we left it broad. Vague and hopeful you may say, but the result proved that it could be done. Long traveled to Stettin on the train, stayed a week in a sailors' lodging-house there, was smuggled on board a Swedish ore ship and got clear away. I wasn't so lucky.

We both approved of travelling by train, but we differed on where to board the thing. Jim, who spoke both German and French very well, proposed to walk to the nearest station to the camp, show the faked French worker's papers he had, buy his ticket and trust to the very ordinariness of the proceeding to carry him through. My own plan was to get as far away from the camp as possible before boarding the train. I picked on Daemmerstadt, which I reckoned I could reach in two nights' walking, lying up in the woods during the intervening day. I was going to travel as a Bulgarian Merchant Navy officer going to join his ship at a Baltic port: my Royal Navy uniform a little altered would pass, I considered, as something almost any German would believe to be the fashion in the Bulgarian Merchant Navy, and our document boys had provided me with a convincing set of papers, including a very outlandish and Balkan-looking one in Cyrillic characters. My major risk was that I might be tackled by someone who knew Bulgarian, but I calculated that the odds were in my favour. For the rest I had four days' rations contributed by our supporters, a button compass which the Germans hadn't found when they picked me up on the beach, some German money and a good sketch-map provided by the Escape Committee.

Jim and I said goodbye hurriedly in the dark of the trees while the hullabaloo of the sham fight was still going on inside the camp. The dogs were barking like fury and some of the goons were shouting, but no one turned a searchlight on our side of the wire. Phase Two of the operation seemed to have succeeded perfectly.

I had memorised my map and had my course very clear in my mind. The first part of the first night's journey would be the worst: it meant steering due east through the pine-forest, off the tracks, for a distance that

I estimated at three hours' walking, until I dropped into a by-road, which I should follow for four or five miles, going roughly north-east, then swing east again to avoid a village, and go by small lanes on a zig-zag course across a wide plain, very thinly inhabited, to another belt of woods, which, I reckoned, I should reach by the first light There I intended to hide and rest The following night I should continue through alternate forest and clearing until about dawn I should come to the railway just south of Daemmerstadt.

I had no illusions about the difficulty of pushing through forest at night, and I had tried to get in as much road-travelling as I thought was safe. I felt I might risk an encounter with peasants or the civil police on the small country roads, for the news of our escape would possibly be late in reaching them and I was cheerfully confident of being able to give a passable imitation of a foreign first mate who'd been on the booze and missed his train, or got out at the wrong station and was setting off to find the right one. I've met a number of such in my time.

There's something to be said for pine-forests. They're infernally dark, but they're much freer of undergrowth than broad-leaved woods. It was not at all easy going on that first leg of my hike and I began to feel that I had underestimated the effect two years of prison fare had had on my strength, but, though it took me nearer five hours than three to reach my road, I did reach it, and, what surprises me more when I look back on it, pretty well at the exact spot where I had reckoned I should. True, I had my compass, but I think I must have had more than my due of what they used to say was the most useful of the Mariner's Aids to Navigation —a bit of damn good luck.

It was a relief to be on the road and to have something to check my position by. I rested a little and ate something, but I dare not take it easy if I was to get into the forest again by daylight. Well, you can imagine the ache of that night hike for yourself: it was worse than any of the trips we ever did together in the old days. Every time I saw a car's headlights I had to creep into an orchard or crouch in the ditch till it was past, and those changes from straight rhythmic slogging became more and more of an agony as the night went on. Once or twice, when I forced myself to get up out of the ditch again, I thought I should never get my legs to work or beat down the burning pain of my blisters again. I can tell you, by the time the sky was turning grey I didn't much care how soon they recaptured me. All I really cared about was stopping walking and getting a drink.

That was my second miscalculation. I had not brought a bottle of water with me so as not to have too much to carry; I had reckoned that in Europe one would never be far from some moderately potable water. It's not so: at least, it seems not to be so in Eastern Europe. I was dodging the villages, of course, and in that sandy region I suppose you don't get brooks and ponds, only wells, and those, naturally, are where the farms are.

I reached my further belt of forest without any very serious alarm, though the sun was well up when I got there. I could see a small farm not far away, with a very tempting-looking cattle-trough in a paddock, but I daren't try to sneak down and have a drink: the day was too far advanced, and even though I could see no one about, there was sure to have been a dog. The best I could do was to limp up into the shade of the pine-trees and crawl about gathering and chewing blades of the pale grass that grew here and there under them.

I rested all that day in the coolest place I could find; I was too parched and sick with fatigue to eat, but I slept—in the uneasy way you do when you are overstrained. The blisters and the aching muscles and the drought of your throat seem to stimulate your brain to activity, while the will, or whatever it is that selects and disciplines thought, is too weary to assert itself. You know the feeling—as if your mind were a cinema projector that has suddenly become animate, taken charge of the proceedings, kicked the operator downstairs and settled down to churn out miles and miles of film for its own devilish amusement, accelerating all the time. I can't remember any of the details of the near-nightmares I had that day in the fringes of that pine-forest, but I can remember the burden of them on my mind, the awful number and speed of them.

Well, perhaps it was that that began it—the great physical strain and the acute anxiety underlying it all. It had not occurred to me that I shouldn't be strong enough. Perhaps I should have stuck with Jim Long.

When it was dusk I pulled myself together and set off again. But this night it was very different. I had lost confidence in my physical ability to carry the thing through, and that was a great shock to me. It was the first time in my life that my body had refused to do something I demanded of it, and the revolt demoralised me. Instead of studying to economise my strength I perversely over-drove myself. And it's no wonder, I suppose, if I got off my course. I had to steer due north, but time and again I came to deep gulleys and ravines that made me wander far off to one side or the other, looking for easy crossing-places; sometimes I saw a light in a clearing and still had determination and courage enough to make a painful detour instead of groping straight towards it and giving myself up.

My memory became confused; the clearings were the only things I had to check my course and progress by and I could not remember how many I had passed or identify them on the map. I used up all my matches trying to study the thing, but I was in such a state of exhaustion and distress that I could scarcely read, let alone reason.

At length, I came into a sandy track on which the moonlight fell clear and strong. It ran somewhat east of north, but the smooth straight way and the light, after the roughness of the dark forest, were such a temptation to me that I could not resist following it. There were wagon-ruts and hoofmarks in the sand. I supposed the track must lead to a farm, but I was beyond caring. I trudged straight along it.

Little by little, I remember, my mind became calmer, and no doubt because of the easier going, and the regular rhythm that was possible, I fell into a kind of automatic action. I began the old, childish trick of repeating something to myself to keep time with my footfalls: meaningless phrases at first, and then, verses. You know the ballad of the Nut Brown Maid? Four lines of that went thump, thump, thump, through my brain, like the dull beat of an engine carrying me on God knows how many miles:

"For an Outlaw this is the law,
That men him take and bind,
And hanged be without pitee,
To waver with the wind."

It's still a wonder to me that under the mechanical, syllabic pounding I made of the verses I did think of the sense sometimes, and I felt a queer, new pathos in them. That coupling of outlawry and pity: I had never thought of that before. The man who wrote that ballad knew that outlaws weren't romantic heroes, all they wanted was pity. Ah, the great cruelty of outlawry in shutting the gates of common men's pity against you.

Had that narrow track led me to a farm, I think I would have leant with my head upon the door and begged for the peasants' pity; but it led to no human habitation.

After a very long time, I felt the dark walls of the forest recede from me. I stopped and became aware that my track had led me up on to a low wide ridge, bare of trees, covered with coarse grass as high as my knees. I have often wondered how much of that scene I really saw that night. I can say what I later knew to be there—or thought I knew. I know exactly how it looked to the eyes I had on the other side—if you understand me—but I'd give anything to be able to recollect precisely what I saw with my real vision—the vision I'm using now. The trouble is, I suppose, that I had been going gradually round the bend all that night. The fatigue and anxiety had found out my flaw and were extending it all the time, until, just about when I reached that open ridge the fissure in my mind was complete. When the earth is opening under you, what decides which side you jump to?

The moonlight seemed bright enough. I thought I saw a long, grassy hog's-back running north-west and south-east. The grass was ungrazed and untrodden, grey under the moon with the white grass-flowers seeming to make a milky shimmer over it. My track had faded away. It occurred to me, I know, that for some time past I had not been following the wagon-ruts, but where they had turned off I could not recall.

I must have advanced to the middle of that broad open ride—fire-lane, or whatever it was—before I stopped, because I could see the forest on the other side, sloping far away, down from the bare ridge. But no real moonlight, in Europe, at least, could have been strong enough to allow me to see those other woods so clearly: it was as if I saw them under a fresh, gay summer's morning, and ah—they were such different woods; not black, monotonous pine-forest, but a fair greenwood of oak and beech and ash and sweet white-flowering hawthorn. It was so enormous a contrast: the difference between night and day, between prison and freedom, between death and life. And looking down from my low ridge, I could just see, over the tops of the nearer trees on that side, a pleasant open glade and in that glade the pale shining of water in a little lake. It was agony to set my legs in motion once more; it felt as if my muscles had turned to stone; but I moved, straight down towards that glint of water.

There was one other thing I saw, and, again, I'd give so much to know which eyes I saw it with; for in my heart I'm still not convinced that the shock I received was real. But all I know is that I did notice something there, between me and those inviting woods, something at odds with experience; a phenomenon that would have been unremarkable enough in a dream and which might yet be not impossible in reality. I felt, as I stumped so painfully down that gentle slope, that in front of me there was a kind of weaker light within the moonlight, some zone of faint luminosity stretching far away on either hand, not straight, like a searchlight beam, but slightly meandering as though it followed the contour of the ridge. I know it's inconsistent with physical laws that so feeble a radiance could be visible in the stronger light of the moon, and yet I swear I was aware of it. Was I outlawed indeed by then, not from man's laws but from Nature's?

Nothing could have kept me from trying to reach that water. Once over the first agony of moving my limbs again, I broke into a stumbling run. I must have gone like a blind man, with my arms stretched out, groping, in front of me, for it was in my hands that I felt the shock first. It was a searing burn across my hands and wrists, then a shock that jarred along every bone in my body and shattered its way upwards, tearing out at the top of my skull; my eyes were pierced by a pain of yellow light, and my body, bereft of all its weight and cohesion, went whirling and spiralling upwards like a gas into the dark.

3

The body, with all its limitations, is a safe and reassuring thing to hold to. I had jumped the gap, no doubt, but I was still aware of the other side. I did not remember it in more or less definite pictures or words, you understand, as you remember the events of last week or one day a year ago, but I was conscious of having existed before, of having had a fairly full and complicated history before I woke up in that clean and comfortable bed. It was my hands that bridged the gap. They were incontrovertibly mine, and they hurt a little. I kept looking at them as they lay on the sheet in front of me, neatly bandaged all over and quite useless to me, but very dear to me.

Apart from the slight pain in my hands I have rarely felt so well and tranquil and at ease in my body as I did that morning when I first began to speculate about where I was. It was not by any means my first day of consciousness. I knew that I had been in that bright and airy room, with its scent of flowers mingling with the fainter odour of drugs and disinfectant and floor-polish, for quite a number of days. The white painted door and window-frame, the pretty curtain and the white wood furniture were all familiar to me, and I knew the faces of my two nurses quite well; they had been looking after me for a long time. It was just that that day I completed a gradual transition from passive perception to active observation.

Had it not been that the nurses were in uniform I should have said that I was in a private house rather than a hospital: the room was too individual in its clean attractiveness for a private ward in any hospital that I have seen. The crockery, the glasses, the dishes and instruments they brought in had not the much-used look such things have in hospitals; and the food was far too good. A light breeze through the open window blew the curtain aside and when the day-nurse propped me up on my pillows in the morning I could see green tree-tops and blue sky, and all day long, from first light to dark, the birds sang loud and near.

I could not use my hands to feed myself; the day-nurse cut up my food and fed me with a spoon; she shaved and washed and bathed me, did everything for me with a professional sureness and cheerful competence.

I had enough experience of nurses not to expect these to gratify my curiosity very fully or easily, but that morning I did ask the day-nurse where I was, and received, of course, the briskly facetious answer: "In bed!" It is a convention, I suppose, among nurses the world over that the most elementary exercise of intelligence by the patient obstructs their task, or else impairs their authority. I tried again, however, and asked her her name.

"It doesn't matter," she said. "You just call me Day Nurse."

The answer, nevertheless, gave me something to work on. She spoke English: extremely good English, but yet with a German accent. That consolidated the bridge across to that very dim and distant other side of the fissure.

I began to reason from my observations methodically and quite calmly. I guessed, of course, what might have happened to me, but it did not alarm me in the least. I jumped to the conclusion, then put it away as a possibility which would be confirmed or not at leisure. I was convinced that I was going to have a great amount of leisure. The impression that I had passed a good few days in semi-consciousness was so strong as to be a certainty; then, I had concrete evidence that an even longer time than I was in any way aware of must have passed since my accident, for the pain in my hands, had diminished to little more than an itching and occasional throbbing, while the one thing that I remembered with extraordinary vividness from across the gap was the intensity of the pain I suffered when I first touched that infernal fence or whatever it was. The burns must have been severe; now they were almost healed; only a long lapse of time could have achieved that. The day after my resumption of observation, to call it so, I looked carefully at my hands while the Day Nurse changed the dressings. It was clear that they had been badly burned, but they were healing remarkably well. The scars, in fact, vanished altogether in a short time. You can see nothing now.

That at any rate gave me some measure of time. Without medical knowledge I could not make a very exact estimate, but common sense and ordinary experience suggested that not less than three or four weeks must have elapsed. The state of my feet when I examined them confirmed that. My blisters were all healed, and I know roughly how long it takes a blister to heal.

To fix my position in space was not so easy. If I was in such an institution as I suspected I could not hope to have straight questions answered. The nurses would fob me off with the most preposterous lies. I should therefore have to rest quietly using my eyes, unhurriedly through the long days, piecing scattered data together until I could draw a true deduction.

Naturally enough I began with my nurses—or rather, Day Nurse. Night Nurse I saw only for a few minutes after sunset and perhaps fleetingly in the early morning. I slept soundly all night and never needed to call her. Day Nurse, then, was obviously German, and just as obviously a professional nurse; yet I could not believe she was a military nursing sister or that she belonged to a public civilian hospital. There was something wrong about her. It was not just that her excellent command of English indicated a better education than nurses usually have—after all, there are plenty of bilingual people about the world. It was her dress, I think. It was too smart, too individual, like the room itself. It was uniform, true, neat and smart and most suggestive of hygiene and asepsis, but at the same time pretty, and worn with a taste and a purpose to look attractive that no hospital, or even private nursing-home that I could conceive, would ever have allowed.

It was certain, too, that no nurses in a public institution would have been able to give me such constant attention or would have treated me with such consideration—within the nursing convention, of course. These two did not seem in the least overworked. In fact, I soon became sure that they had no other patient but me. Day Nurse was able to spend unlimited time with me, and I never heard a bell ring about the place. Indeed, beyond the voices of my nurses, their soft steps on the polished wooden floor and the song of birds outside my window, I heard no noise whatever of the world for some time.

I think it was that unnatural silence of the first few days that convinced me that I was in a private mental home. I settled on that identification of the place and set myself to discover, if I could, by the same process of observation and deduction, how I had come there, and why I was being treated like a private patient of considerable means instead of as a prisoner of war, for, you understand, there was no true amnesia: I knew all the time that I was a British Naval officer and I could remember my name and my ship and my prison camp.

Questioning Day Nurse was no use at all, though I tried as subtly as I knew. She wasn't taciturn, but she had a peculiar gift for appearing bright and talkative while saying almost nothing outside the things to do with her job of looking after my bodily needs.

Only one fact emerged: the name of the place, she told me, was Hackelnberg. That gave me matter for a day's reflection. It was a satisfying, concrete fact, but it led me on to no deduction, or rather, it led me only to another fact without explaining it. I found, to my great pleasure, that by deliberate concentration I could recall, little by little, the whole of the sketch-map that I had had from the Escape Committee, and, lying there, seeing the map behind my closed eyes, I assured myself that there was no such name as Hackelnberg on it. I had then, it seemed, been taken a good way, more than forty miles, which was the radius of my map, from Oflag XXIX Z.

There seemed no point in trying to find out whether Day Nurse knew that I was a British prisoner of war. I had been speaking English ever since I regained consciousness, and had no doubt spoken it in my coma. The Doctor would have told the police; the Intelligence officers would have had a look at me—I could imagine them, a couple of S.S. boys, no doubt, going through my few belongings, my papers, the map, the button compass which would tell them the whole story, then conferring with the Doctor and finally accepting his diagnosis of my mental state and leaving me.

Yes, but leaving me to whose care? Whose was this place? Why should the managers or the owners treat and care for me? Such places are not generally run by philanthropists. I revolved this question for hours, and the end of it was only to bring a shade of doubt into my first belief that the place was a private mental home. If it was, then the likeliest explanation of my being taken in was that my case must seem to the Doctor to present some peculiarly interesting features and he was keeping me and treating me out of scientific curiosity. But I did admit the 'if,' now. If it was not a mental home it could only be the house of some rich person endowed with the eccentricity of compassion—and possessing some considerable pull with the authorities; perhaps an invalid himself, or herself: that would explain both the presence of the trained nurses and their un-institutional air.

I have said 'rich person'; well, I was aware of material wealth in the whole atmosphere. There was nothing worn or shabby about the room; nurses, to be so smartly dressed, so very well groomed, must be well paid; the spotless cleanliness of the floor and high polish of the waxed wooden furniture betokened an ample staff of servants, and I knew that the nurses themselves did none of the cleaning. In fact, though I had not consciously observed it until I began to reason in this fashion, I knew who did the cleaning.

I had seen him in the early mornings—a stout young man, silent and very busy on hands and knees, polishing away at the shining floor. After what I call my full awakening I observed him more closely. He was fleshy and well-fed, and though he kept his head averted most of the time, I had an occasional glimpse of his features as I lay in bed. They were smooth and blank, and he had close-cropped brown hair and pale blue eyes; the thickness of his body, his dumbness and calflike look, his quadrupedal posture, all gave him the air of some strong, mild domestic animal—a bullock or a plough-ox; and that was emphasised by the way he was dressed that particular early morning when I paid attention to him. He wore no shirt, only a pair of rather tight trousers of some good, substantial-looking brown stuff, and on his feet a pair of good shoes which appeared to be made all of rubber, or perhaps of some kind of artificial leather that was new to me. It looked strong, supple and comfortable.

I spoke to him that morning while the nurse was out, but he paid no more attention to me than a bullock would have done. It was not difficult to guess, all the same, what he must be. A German of his age could not have been employed as a domestic servant: he would have been in the army, or making munitions. Had this been a military institution anywhere one would have said at once he was a P.O.W. But I was in Germany, I knew the German system of drafting what we called slave-labour from the occupied countries and making it available to private employers. This fellow was clearly a Slav prisoner of war hired out in service. He had the right *muzhik* look.

Observing his shoes and the stuff of his trousers so closely led me to study the other fabrics and materials surrounding me, and I found some matter for wonder there. I cannot claim to know much about fabrics, or even to have noticed them much in my life before, but all these struck me as being extremely good and costly. The pyjamas I had on, for instance, were silk—or some stuff I could not distinguish from silk; the sheets were of the very finest linen; the coverlet, silk again; the china I ate off was most delicate; the glass—well, I peered at the tumbler, medicine-glass, and other things on the table beside my bed and came to the conclusion that they were not glass at all, but some admirably manufactured plastic, capable of being as finely cut and polished as glass, but unbreakable. I proved that by pushing one of the more delicate vessels off the table with my bandaged hand on to the floor. It suffered no hurt.

Such little things impress you. They are such convincing evidence of a highly developed industry, of abundant material wealth which enables people to keep all their domestic equipment new and perfect. The Germans, of course, had a reputation in industrial chemistry, in plastics and synthetic fabrics, and so on, but it was disconcerting to find such things so abundant in civilian life after nearly four years of war.

The furniture and the floor of the room, at any rate, were not made from coal-tar or milk or wood-pulp— but of natural wood with the beauty and variety of the forest in their grain. The timber had been chosen and worked by people who loved it. I began to feel I knew something of the character of the owner of this place of Hackelnberg. He was rich, obviously; perhaps an old Junker or one of the princes of the old Empire whom the Nazis found it politic to leave alone; one who was not only able to buy the best products of the factories, but who also had the taste to combine them with the best of country craftsmanship using woodland materials. He would be a lover of forest things.

Well, all that, you may say, was as much fancy as deduction. Sherlock Holmes, no doubt, would have done much better with the data provided by one room and three people, but I flatter myself that the broad lines were pretty accurate.

I had my first positive confirmation from the source where I least looked for it: from Night Nurse, to whom I scarcely spoke more than to say good evening or good morning. But it was an odd thing that got it out of her.

I have mentioned that the extraordinary quietness of the place was one of the things that formed the basis of my reasonings. It fitted the other explanation, too, of course: that I was a guest, a prisoner-guest if you like, in a country house. The property was obviously a large one. How large, I had no idea, for even when, in the nurses' absence, I crept out of bed to the window, I could see no distance at all: the trees just outside were too tall and their foliage too thick to give me any view except of their own green complexity. There was, however, no noise of traffic, not even the most distant sound of a car horn or an engine whistle. I did not even hear an aeroplane, and that, in Germany in 1943, struck me as peculiar. True enough, the Third Reich at the point of expansion it had then reached was a much wider land than England; airfields would not necessarily be so thick on the ground in Eastern Germany as they were at that time in East Anglia, for example. And I supposed Hackelnberg was far enough east to be out of range of our own bombers; there was certainly no black-out curtain in my room, no precautions about showing lights were ever taken, and you could never have suspected from anything in the nurses' conversation that they so much as knew that Germany was at war. That was deliberate, of course: part of the business of nursing me and avoiding topics that might excite me. Whenever I mentioned the war Day Nurse pretended a complete misunderstanding of what I was saying, told me I was not to bother my head with old past things and tried to interest me in the flowers.

Then about a week after this full awakening of mine I began to hear things. My hands were almost completely healed and I was perfectly well in myself. I wanted to get up; lying in bed all day began to bore me. The result was that I no longer slept soundly all night.

At first I thought the sounds were dream-sounds, for I heard them in a doze, slept again and only recollected them in the morning. They were such remote, isolated sounds, so unconnected with the restricted life going on round me. They were notes of a horn, sounded at long intervals, each one as lonely in the pitch dark and utter silence, as one single sail on a wide sea. I've heard bugles in the dark and loneliness of the sea and I've heard an English huntsman's horn, and I know how sometimes their music can tighten like a hand-grip on your heart. But these notes were different. I could not picture the scene where they were being sounded, I could only feel the profound melancholy, the wildness and strangeness of them; they spoke through the dullness of my half-sleep with a most desolating sorrow and pain.

I remembered their sadness long into the cheerful day, and I found myself listening for them the next night, wide awake in the dark, waiting for them, yet hoping I should not hear them.

One night I heard them before ever I had gone to sleep. There could be no question of a dream then. It was a light night with the moon near full and only a few small islands of white cloud. I slipped out of bed and listened at the open window. There was some wind and that played with the horn notes, lifting them to me one moment, then changing and bearing them far away; that surging and dying seemed to give their music a different quality this night The sadness and pain were still there, but the wildness was dominant; the horn seemed to be roving about the woods, beating back and forth, questing, calling, sometimes with a stirring fierceness, sometimes with the long, withdrawing note of failure.

The night was full of noises. The forest was as restless as the ocean. The wind stirred the beeches outside my window; the trees conversed in a multitude of tongues; a whole woodland orchestra was playing, with the horn leading. I could fancy all sorts of voices and instruments within that wild discourse; imagination could turn the whine of swaying branches into the whimper of hounds and the sudden loud shuddering rustle of leaves in a gust could be the racing patter of their feet. I leaned there a long time, listening, intent on the horn above all the other sounds, and I felt a strange disturbance of spirits increasing within me; it was not the sadness the horn had induced in me before, but a nervousness, an apprehension—that enfeebling sense of danger you may have sometimes before you have realised from what quarter, by what weapon you are threatened.

I listened until the horn had died far away and my ear could no longer distinguish it above the soughing and sighing of the uneasy trees, then I crept back into bed and lay for a long time, looking at the moon-lit square of my window, listening still for the notes to sound again, but at length I fell asleep.

Before it was well light I was out of bed again, torn suddenly from sleep by the horn very loud and close. The wind had fallen now, the moon had set; the morning was quiet and grey; and then I heard the loud horn ringing arrogantly through the grave twilight of the dawn. The note of triumph was insistent. I leaned out and tried to pierce the screen of trees with my vision; the oft-repeated blasts were passing through the woods not far from my window, passing away to somewhere beyond my room to the right.

Out of the corner of my eye I caught a glimpse of a white form gliding through the dusk of my room and I gave a great start of fright before I recognised Night Nurse.

"Go back to bed!" she whispered, making the low, urgent tone sound more peremptory than any I had heard her use before. She moved between me and the window and stood with her back to the opening, as though to prevent me throwing myself out, and all the time I could see that she was listening intently to those prancing, exultant notes of the horn, diminishing now as they passed on through the forest.

"What is it?" I asked, when I had obeyed her and covered myself with the sheet again. Utterly unexpectedly she gave me a straight, serious answer:

"It is the Count coming home."

It was a true answer, I was certain; she had forgotten for the moment that I was her patient and had let slip into her voice an expression of just that vague alarm that I myself had felt when listening to the horn the night before.

"The Count?" I asked. "Who is the Count?" She came and looked down at me, so that I could just make out her features in the grey light from the window.

She murmured something in German, then explained in English:

"Count Johann von Hackelnberg."

"And who is he?" I persisted, being determined to make the most of this opportunity when she seemed to have been startled into treating me as a sane person. But she paused and considered me before replying, as if my ignorance had reminded her that I was not normal after all; still, she did answer:

"Well, he is the Reich Master Forester."

"Is he?" I said. "I thought Marshal Goering was that."

I might have mentioned the name of our ship's cat for all the recognition she showed. She had got over her lapse into sincerity, I saw, and was back again in this pretence that the contemporary world did not exist—the pretence which was part of my treatment, I supposed.

She looked quite blank and repeated the name absently once or twice, evidently thinking of something entirely different. Then with an effort she became brisk and shook up my pillows.

"Come now!" she ordered. "You must go to sleep. You must not wake so early. It is not good for you." And she went smartly out of the room.

I reviewed the whole matter in the sunlight with some satisfaction. I had at last got something definite. It was news to me that Hermann Goering had divested himself of one of his functions, but it was more than likely that we should never have heard of that event in Oflag XXIX Z. What was settled was that I was the guest of the Reich Master Forester, and that seemed to me to explain more than it left unexplained. But what a queer character the Graf von Hackelnberg must be to go a-hunting in the forest by moonlight. A breakneck business, I should have thought; then I began to recall tales of our English eccentrics of the eighteenth century. It might well have been not a hunt I heard, but a drunken ride, a wild spree by young Nazis full of wine, with the old Count winding them on with his hunting horn. It was a plausible picture, but it did not quite convince me. The horn had sounded too often; it had gone on too long, and the nurse had not been shocked in the way she would have been by the drunken wildness of a gang of young bloods; that home-coming horn was familiar to her; she was frightened of something she knew very well.

4

Day Nurse bustled in with my breakfast, and I noticed a distinct change in her manner. She was taut with self-importance and insufferably authoritarian. I was not greatly surprised, when, having whisked away my breakfast things and rearranged the speckless vessels on my bedside-table, she announced that the Doctor was coming to see me. She made me nervous by the exaggerated importance she gave to the visit, but, as if to console me for her brusqueness, a little before the hour she confided that he might let me get up if he was satisfied by his examination. I was shaved and washed, my pyjamas were changed, the bed fresh-made, the dustless room dusted, new flowers were brought in and the shining floor given a super shine by the broad-backed serf who went at the job like clockwork. Finally Day Nurse removed the dressings from my hands, produced the steriliser and various bright instruments and then, as a light footfall sounded outside, stood to rigid attention at the foot of my bed. The Doctor came in humming a jaunty tune, glanced quickly round the room and addressed Day Nurse, who seemed frozen there, with a glazed look in her eyes. I'd seen nurses in England overdo the yessir-nosir business with a surgeon, and I'd seen a little of German discipline, but this out-prussianed them all. A quartermaster answering an Admiral on an inspection day was nothing to Day Nurse; she looked as brittle and unbending as a figure of glass and the short replies came snapping out like whip-cracks. The Doctor was anything but officer-like. He lounged, rather than stood, and he looked the nurse up and down as he questioned her with more of a lazy interest in her figure and dress than in what she was saying. He was a young man, with a pasty face, intelligent-looking enough, but self-indulgent and domineering. He was dressed in white trousers and a cream silk shirt with a bright silk handkerchief tied loosely round his throat. I could imagine him having leaned his tennis-racket just outside the door.

After hearing Day Nurse's report and giving a glance at my temperature chart, he moved over and looked at me, knitted his brows for a second and then waggled his head and looked rather pleased with himself. His examination was perfunctory; he listened to my heart, felt my pulse, lifted my lids and peered into my eyes, and, after a final hard stare at my hands, straightened up and said in very good English:

"You can get up now. Come and have a chat in my office."

Day Nurse thawed the moment he was out of the room and in her relief that the ordeal was over she was almost gushing. She brought me a rich brocade dressing gown and a pair of slippers made of the same soft synthetic leather that I had seen the Slav servant wearing.

For all I felt so well, my knees, of course, were like water from lying so long in bed and I was glad of Day Nurse's arm. It was the first time I had been outside my room and I had something to do to control my eagerness to see what the place looked like. I had no more than a hurried glimpse of my surroundings, for the Doctor's office was close by, across a broad verandah. I saw, however, that my room was at the corner of a spacious, one-storey wooden building raised above the ground by a high brick base. The forest came very close; there was no garden, only the natural lawns of the woodland in the openings of the trees.

The Doctor's room was more shaded by the trees than my own. The light that came in was leaf-green, yet the effect of the white-painted walls and the high polish on all the woodwork was such that the room looked light. It seemed half study, half surgery; bookcases and instrument cabinets alternated round the walls and a vast wooden desk stood in the middle. The Doctor invited me to sit in an easy chair beside the desk and swivelled his desk-chair round to face me, dismissing the nurse with a nod.

I suppose I talked far more than a prisoner of war ought that morning. After the baffling 'humouring' to which I had been subjected by the nurses it was a great relief to talk to someone who appeared, at least, to treat me as a sane and normal person. It was naive of me, no doubt, but it did not occur to me that he was encouraging me to talk in order to study me; I believed that he just wanted the pleasure of a chat. He gave me the impression of not having enough work to do, of being bored and glad to see a stranger. I forgot how much he must have known about me already. I don't know how many canons of security I offended against, but, with his prompting, and under the stimulus of his interest, I told him the whole story of my escape, concealing only the fact that Jim Long had escaped with me. He drew with a pencil on a pad in front of him while was talking, but took no notes. When I had finished he gave me a long stare. It was only then, I think, when I looked back into his eyes that I became aware of some kind of calculation in his manner, something not so easy and trustworthy as I had thought at first.

"Tell me this," I blurted out. "Why don't you hand me over to the police? I've admitted that I'm a British prisoner."

"The police?" he repeated thoughtfully. "It is not necessary. The Master Forester has jurisdiction in the Reich forest."

"But I'm a prisoner of war," I persisted. "I should be under military law."

"*Ja, ja,*" he said. "I understand. There is no hurry. We must get you well first."

I realised, angrily, that this was the same vein of 'humouring' the lunatic that the nurses had practised.

I said defiantly:

"You think I'm mad, don't you?"

"My dear fellow," he answered, and something jarred on me in the glib way he brought the phrase out in his German accent, "my dear fellow, I don't think you're insane at all. Not that I should care much if you were. Your case interested me physiologically. You were affected by Bohlen Rays. They are usually fatal, but you have responded to my treatment. I am pleased with you. From my point of view you are cured, you need only a little time and some exercise to recover the use of your muscles completely."

"But you think I'm unbalanced," I insisted. "Even though you're not interested, you're a doctor; you know when a person's mad. Am I?" He looked out of the window and drew down the corners of his mouth, seeming to find my question irrelevant or impossible to answer. Then in a bored, offhand way, he said:

"There's bound to be some cerebral disturbance. A temporary amnesia would be normal and some kind of delusions could be expected. In your case it seems to take the form of believing that you are living in a former period of history. I suppose you have read a good deal of history, about the War of German Rights and so forth, haven't you?"

"History?" I said, bewildered. "Yes...."

He interrupted me airily.

"I should not worry. It will pass." He looked at me with very much the same indolent appreciation in his eyes as when he had surveyed Day Nurse, interested in nothing but my physical state. "What does it matter if it doesn't?" he asked. "You have the use of your body again. I don't know that you'll find anyone particularly interested in your mind here."

Even though I had by now seen through the sham geniality of his first manner, the brutality of this remark astonished me. Puzzled and alarmed though I was at what he said about my delusion, I was convinced in my own mind that I was sane and I determined to meet his brutality with composure.

"I'm not so conceited, Doctor, as to imagine that my mind is of much interest to anybody but myself," I said. "But I should like to thank you for taking such very good care of my body; it feels quite well now and I think my only worry is what you intend to do with it now you've repaired it. Am I to be treated as a prisoner of war, or not?"

He put his elbows on the desk, propped his chin on his folded hands and arched his brows, looking at me with a certain disquieting relish.

"You know, I like you," he said. "I find your conversation refreshing. Besides, I think you are probably a good listener and it will be excellent for me to practice my English a little. I have no idea what the Graf intends to do with you, but in my own little hospital here I am Der Fuehrer—and in case your period doesn't come as far up to modern times as that, that means God—and as I like your company I shall keep you here as long as possible. You have no idea how depressing it is for a solitary intellectual surrounded entirely by sportsmen and slaves. I am sure you will stimulate me to make a great many observations about this establishment, and luckily your—er—infirmity will enable me to express them with comparative safety. You may keep your room until I need it for another casualty, but I beg that you will honour my own table. I shall try to show you something of the estate as opportunity offers, but I must warn you against going out by yourself, particularly at night. It would grieve me very much to have my first real success with the anti-Bohlen Ray treatment unprofessionally dissected by the Graf's hounds or those other creatures that he keeps."

He rose, and coming swiftly round clapped me on the shoulder, grinning down at me.

"So, Herr Lieutenant, accept the fortune of war like a soldier of those old heroic times you live in, and share a piece of venison and a bottle of Bordeaux with your enemy at half-past twelve precisely. Ach, though!" he exclaimed. "I must get you something to wear. Your own clothes have gone to the incinerator, I believe."

He bent and spoke softly into a small apparatus on his desk. While he was occupied I got up and looked at the fine electric clock on the bookcase to which he had pointed when he invited me to lunch. It was a handsome instrument, comprising not only a clock but a thermometer and barometer, and it exhibited certain additional figures in small illuminated apertures which I did not at once understand. Then, I saw that one combination must give the day of the month. It was evidently the twenty-seventh of July. But under this was the isolated figure '102.'

The Doctor came across while I was peering at this.

"So," he said. "You admire my chronometer? As an officer of the old-time Navy that should interest you. But what puzzles you about it?"

I pointed to the small figure '102.'

"*Ach, ja,*" he said. "The year also. Hardly necessary, one would have thought."

"The year?" I repeated, staring at him.

He threw back his head and laughed aloud, then apologised with exaggerated courtliness.

"Alas, it is so difficult to be consistent when two people are living in different centuries at the same time. Forgive me, I should explain that I—solely for purposes of practical convenience, of course—subscribe to the convention that we are living in the hundred and second year of the First German Millenium as fixed by our First

Fuehrer and Immortal Spirit of Germanism, Adolf Hitler."

5

It amazes me now that I preserved so unruffled a faith in my own sanity all the time I was at Hackelnberg. Perhaps I did it by achieving a kind of suspension of judgment: I was in a set of curious circumstances for which I could find no immediate and satisfying explanation, but there must be an explanation and I felt I should eventually arrive at it by patient observation and reasoning. I felt an immense patience in myself. Perhaps that was a legacy of the prison camp; you can't plan and execute a tunnelling project without having or acquiring patience. Still, it is surprising how easy I found it to leave this whole matter of chronology in abeyance. The Doctor believed he was living a hundred years after the war, I believed I was living in it: time would show which of us was right. Time, yes, and space too. If I could go about a bit and see the other people at Hackelnberg, I felt I should soon know one way or the other.

Yet, of course, I reasoned from my inner conviction, even supposing the Doctor was right, that would not prove that I was mad. The Doctor thought I was suffering from some harmless delusion, but there would be another possible explanation: might not my unconsciousness have covered a century of time? Might I not have slept in the forest now called Hackelnberg for a hundred years like Rip Van Winkle in the Catskills?

Well, you'll probably say there was no doubt about my state of mind if I could consider such an explanation seriously. But what is a man to think when he feels so well, so balanced, so sane, and above all, when his senses are working so perfectly and he is taking such a lively interest in everything round him? Never in my life had I been so intent on observing and memorising everything I saw. I tell you, my memories of what I saw at Hackelnberg, what I felt and did there, are more vivid and real to me than anything else in my whole life.

It was all so real, and—though it's a queer thing to say, seeing what happened—so interesting.

I don't mean that all the discoveries were pleasant. They were not by any means. In fact, they would have appalled me if I had kept leaping back and forth across the time-gap, as it were, to look at them with the eyes of 1943. But I didn't do that. I accepted the apparent history of the last hundred years as known to Hackelnberg, and later, escape meant not escape in time, but escape in space. The problem was to get across that fence of rays again.

After all, facing it honestly, could a humble Lieutenant of the Royal Navy in mid-1943 have been blamed for admitting, to himself, that Germany might win the war? It looked uncommonly as if she'd already won it, to us, in our prison camp. And if she had won it, and a hundred years had consolidated her victory, then the leaders of the Nazis were literally lords of the world. And the Nazi bosses, as we all knew, had in them the makings of most fantastic tyrants, whose extravagances of despotism when the world was theirs would make the annals of Roman Emperors and Mongol Khans read like the minutes of a Parish Meeting.

Unfortunately, if you look at it that way, I landed in a secluded part of the German Empire, a private preserve from which I had no chance of observing what had happened to the world in general. I could only deduce the world-wide and absolute power of the lords of the Master Race.

In practice, I was the prisoner-patient—guest, he chose to call it—of the Herr Professor-Doktor Wolf von Eichbrunn, but I was left in no doubt that the ultimate disposal of my person was at the discretion of the Master Forester, Count Johann von Hackelnberg. I did not much like the way all the hospital staff lowered their voices and cringed slightly when they spoke the Count's name. I remembered the Night Nurse's frightened whisper when she caught me listening to the horn.

Only the Doctor spoke lightly of the Master Forester, but I could detect a real uneasiness under his affected superiority and, also, when he mocked the rigid discipline he enforced in his own place and blamed it on the system, his insincerity was patent.

After my first meal at his table I found myself paying less attention to his self-centred remarks and studying the staff. I had discovered that only half the girls were trained nurses, the other six were housemaids, though what work they had to do beyond waiting at his table was not easy to see, since there were about the place at least a dozen men—young men, all extraordinarily similar in build and appearance to the fellow who cleaned my room. Two of them used to bring in the dishes from the kitchen to the Doctor's dining-room and then stand by the sideboard while two maids took over and served us at table. They were always naked to the waist, so that I could observe their well-fed, sleek bodies; the livery trousers they wore of green or brown stuff were so tight as to mould their haunches and legs; they all looked as if they were running to fat, and were only kept in condition by a lot of hard work, though none of them seemed above twenty-two or so. I noticed that each wore a thin collar of bright metal round his neck.

"They are cheaper than machines," was the Doctor's comment when I said something about them. "Besides, the Graf has a prejudice against mechanisation. He concedes a point or two on the apparatus of destruction, but he would rather give me three slaves than one vacuum-cleaner."

"What are they, what nationality are they?" I asked. He shrugged. "Slavs, I suppose. I've never really gone into their breeding. They seem to me very much just lumps of undifferentiated Under-Race. They are breeding them extensively in the South Russian Gau nowadays. I suppose your little lapse from contemporaneity does not permit you to be acquainted with the discoveries of Wessler in mechanically induced conception and the application of the Roeder-Schwab process for the acceleration of growth? It's pleasant, isn't it, to think that the father of both those oxen there was perhaps the same piece of copper-wire—and what age would you estimate them?"

I guessed about twenty-two.

"Not more than fifteen, and twelve more likely. Precocious infants, aren't they? But the precocity is physical only, fortunately, I should say."

"I don't know that I should feel very happy to have the command of twelve bulky men with the minds of children, nevertheless," I remarked.

He sniggered. "Oh, some physical precautions are taken. In time, I've no doubt, they'll breed them without unnecessary organs, but at present the breeders trim off the ones that might cause trouble, soon after birth. You observe also that they don't talk? The Graf thinks it a convenience to have a small operation done on their vocal cords before we get them."

I looked from the serfs to the two young girls in smart green and white uniforms who were waiting on us and asked if they too were slaves.

"Indeed, no!" he answered, eyeing them with pride. "Pure German maidens. The Graf uses a good number of slave-girls, but I would not have the trouble of them. If you have properly educated German children discipline is automatic. If any girl breaks a rule the others at once report it. Selbstzeuchtigung! The culprit usually anticipates that and reports her own fault and proposes the proper punishment." He let his eyes slide across the two trim young maids and added complacently, with a suggestion of lip-smacking in his tone: "They know better than to propose too little, too!"

The more I lived in that polished, aseptic place, in that atmosphere of rigidly disciplined slavery, the more interesting the night-hunting Count seemed to me with his hints of eccentricity. From time to time I still heard his horn in the woods and it still had that strange, disturbing and vaguely alarming effect on me; but so far I had seen no sign of him or the company he kept. I knew, from walking round the hospital building daily with one or other of the nurses, that the Schloss, as they called it, lay a short distance through the trees to the north of us, but as I was never allowed out alone, or without one of the dumb serfs hovering within sight, I made no attempt to cross the belt of woodland between. The Doctor had told me what would happen to the girl if she lost sight of me.

The best I could do was to protest to von Eichbrunn that this limited exercise was not enough for me. He countered with the reply that it was as much as he ever took. But it was so tantalising to have the wide forest at one's door and be denied the freedom of it that I persisted, until, finally, one day, after hearing me with some discontent and impatience, he resigned himself.

"I can see," he said, "that if I don't satisfy your curiosity you'll do something very foolish like trying to run off by yourself. I suppose you're revolving some romantic piece of Anglo-Saxon adventurousness, aren't you? And if that's so I can't expect either your old-world feelings of chivalry towards my maedels or a regard for your own skin to deter you. Well, if nothing will satisfy but to see Hans von Hackelnberg it is better that I should take you to the Schloss. Better for you, my friend," he said, spacing his words with great emphasis, "better for you to see him than for him to see you."

He spilt his wine—the red Bordeaux—I remember, as he said the last words, and it seemed to me that the action was deliberate. It might have been a libation he poured there, a prayer to the gods to interpose between him and an evil power; it might have been a dramatic trick of rhetoric, whose force I could not mistake as I gazed at the red pool glinting on the wood between us. One of the maids swiftly mopped it up with a napkin and he pushed aside his chair and laughed uneasily.

"*Ach*, well," he said, after a pause, in a lighter and friendlier tone. "I will arrange it. *Ja*, I will tell you what. The day after tomorrow the Count is entertaining the Gauleiter of Gascony and some of his friends. They will make a tour of the forest and do some shooting. The Schloss will be empty all morning. *Ja*, I can show you the Schloss, perhaps also some game; you will not have seen such game as the Count preserves for his guests. Then, later, perhaps—but I do not promise, mind,—I will let you have a look at Hans von Hackelnberg in his hall."

6

Von Eichbrunn was as good as his word. I was roused very early the morning after next, and before I had finished putting on the suit of forest clothes he had sent in to me I heard him calling me from the verandah. It was a fine fresh morning; the scent of the forest was intoxicatingly strong and sweet. I had heard no horns in the night; my sleep had been unbroken and dreamless; now the loud bird-song, the awakening quiver of the woods, the strengthening light on leaves and boles and grassy glades, exhilarated me.

The Doctor was dressed for the forest in a pair of close-fitting dark green trousers with broad gold braid, half-boots of suede-like material, and a jerkin that looked like a doe-skin richly frogged and ornamented with gold. He had a green velvet cap sporting a heron's feather on his head and swinging from a belt a long dirk or hunting sword with an ivory hilt. The suit he had lent me was after the same style, but plain.

He led me along one of the little paths winding away from the hospital, and I noticed he had caused two of the Slav serfs to follow us.

We had not gone more than a quarter of a mile when we came in sight of the first buildings of the Schloss. It is difficult for me to describe the place because I never had a general a view of it. In fact, it would be impossible to see it as a whole, for the forest grew not only close up to it but within its courts and alleys and arched over it in places like a tent. It was far from being a castle, as I had imagined it. The buildings were all low, half-timbered or built entirely of wood, exceedingly irregular in design, as if the architects had been obliged not to fell a single tree, but to make their plans conform to the shape and site of all the existing glades and open spaces in the area. In some places, indeed, enormous beeches or oaks were actually knitted into the fabric of the buildings, and there were turrets and little chambers contrived like nests among their spreading boughs.

There was something curiously secret about the place in this still and early morning. It was not simply that there was no one about: I had been prepared for that. I think it was that the austere, bright smartness of the hospital had led me to expect something of the same style in the Schloss, and instead I found a mediaeval waywardness, a fantastic crabbedness and contortion. These low, rambling buildings with their gables and dormers, their overhangs and nooks, odd windows and recessed doorways, seemed to have writhed in and out of the forest trees of their own accord, to have sought the shade and privacy of the groves like woodland beasts. They were forest dwellings through and through, their beams and boards, their lime and plaster, their grey foundation-stones and doorsills, were native to the earth about them. They were as sylvan as an Iroquois teepee or backwoodsman's cabin; and yet they were not rude. There was a kind of sly art in their construction; their baffling irregularity, their flight, as it were, from expected proportions and planes, had yet a Gothic cunning and mastery in it. We penetrated into a maze of courts and narrow walks, moss-grown and cobbled, tip-toed through pannelled passages and oaken galleries, and the fancy grew on me that we were stealing through a deserted and lost little German town of the Middle Ages which the forest had overgrown while time, by a miracle, had allowed it to defy ruin.

Von Eichbrunn spoke little and in a low voice, answering few of my questions, dropping only the briefest word of explanation as he showed me dwellings and dormitories, kitchens, kennels and stables. I would have liked to linger and look at the hounds and horses, at the carriages in the coach-houses and at the racks of old hunting arms and gear in some of the galleries, but he hurried me on, nervously anxious, I thought, to be out in the open, or the comparative open, of the forest again. So, I could see only that the Master Forester of the Reich appeared to keep a variety of hounds: one pack of stag-hounds of the black and white French St Hubert breed; some bloodhounds and some great creatures like boar-hounds, short-haired, brindled, tremendously strong and ferocious as tigers, which hurled themselves with savage snarling at the bars of their kennels as we passed. I have never seen such villainy, such determination to attack, even in the police dogs that our prison-camp guards kept. The Doctor glided by, as far from their fangs and their pale, glaring eyes as he could get.

The fury we had drawn on ourselves seemed to unnerve the Doctor so much that he forgot his way. We had come out, beyond the boar-hounds' kennel, into a little court, dimmed by the foliage of overhanging trees, out of which ran several dark little passages. Von Eichbrunn turned about, hesitating which one to take, then glanced back and made a questioning sign to one of the serfs who had followed us. Before the man could respond, a clear voice called challengingly from one of the passages. Von Eichbrunn started, then, with an unconvincing smile, dived into the passage, pulling me with him. He turned almost immediately through a doorway into a long, light room, of which one window gave on to the court we had left, while others, high up, looked to the blue sky through gaps in the tree-tops.

I saw that it was a young man who had challenged us; a youth dressed much as the Doctor was dressed, except that he had laid aside his jerkin and was in his shirtsleeves. Observing him from behind the Doctor, I thought him almost too perfect a specimen of what we used to consider the typical young Nazi to be true: not heavily built, but with a suggestion of the bruiser in his figure and pose; hair and lashes so fair he would have passed for albino but for his grey eyes; a face which, in the moment of haughty enquiry before he recognised von Eichbrunn, was a mask of exaggerated arrogance and cold authority, but which, when he briefly returned the Doctor's greeting, looked only selfish and sneering, with a suggestion of careless brutality about the eyes and mouth.

They spoke in German, the Doctor evidently explaining something about me. I felt the young man's eyes on me and carefully avoided them, looking round the room instead.

It appeared to be a keeper's or huntsman's room, stored with a strange variety of equipment, all having the air of being in use, well-kept, neatly arranged and ready to hand. Even the boar-spears standing in their racks by the wall were bright and serviceable-looking: that was the oddity of the place—so much of the gear did not fit into von Eichbrunn's chronology at all. Why was there a row of cross-bows, their steel parts shining, their strings new and strong, lances and short swords, and, in a farther corner, arranged on wooden stands, what looked like several suits of armour, though rather made of tough leather, or material resembling it, than of steel? The Graf von Hackelnberg seemed to be a determined mediaevalist. There was one concession to modernity: a stand of short, single-barrelled guns of very wide bore, far wider than one of our eight-bores or anything I have seen used for wild-fowling; and there were stacks of metal boxes which, I guessed contained cartridges. Besides these there was hunting gear of the sort which I suppose time has modified only a little: hound leashes and couples, collars and whips.

There was a profusion of stuff in the room and I had time to observe only the more obvious things; I noticed, however, that though there were no trophies, such as

stags' heads, foxes' masks, and so on, that one might
expect to see in such a room, there was a number of
skins, or parts of skins, all apparently of the same sort,
hanging on the wall at the farther end near the strange
suits of armour. They were not displayed as trophies but
hanging on a row of pegs. I could see the down-dangling
tails, and I thought they looked like leopard skins; but
perhaps they were brindled wild-cat skins. It seemed
likely enough that wild-cats might be fairly common
vermin in a great forest like Hackelnberg.

One other thing I noticed: The fair-haired youth had
been standing at a long broad table in the middle of the
room, doing something with some gear among the litter
of the things that strewed it. He laid down the object he
had been working on as he moved a little aside to talk to
the Doctor; it was some small piece of metal apparatus
and he had been working on it with a file. Edging a little
closer, I saw that it was a queer-looking arrangement of
steel hooks, arranged like fingers of a hand, and just
about the size of my hand, or a bit less. It was, in fact,
remotely suggestive of a steel gauntlet without any cuff.
There were several such things lying on the table, one or
two fitted somehow with straps. I suppose that in
another moment I should have got close enough to pick
the thing up and examine it in my hands, but the Doctor
took me by the arm and led me out with him.

He seemed to have allayed the suspicions of the
young keeper, for he went out with us and chatted
amiably enough to von Eichbrunn, though he did not
address a single word to me. No doubt he knew nothing
but German, and though, you know, I can just stumble
along in German and understand it if it is spoken slowly
enough, I had never let von Eichbrunn know that.

The keeper accompanied us across the little court
and let us out into a park-like area of well-spaced trees.
Here I caught a glimpse of much the biggest single
building I had yet seen. Nearly hidden by the trees as it

was, I could make out that it was a great, stone-built hall, Gothic in style, steep-roofed, pinnacled and turreted, complexly ornamented like a fanciful reproduction of some sixteenth-century Rathaus in the Rhineland.

I would have liked to go close and look at it, but again, von Eichbrunn steered me away: what the keeper was about to show us lay in another direction. He led us by little paths between hedges of clipped forest trees among a group of corrals—his game-farm, I supposed, for the enclosures were stocked with numbers of very tame roes, fallow-deer and red-deer, all does and hinds, fawns and calves, as far as I could see. They came running from among the trees and bushes at his call and fed from his hand, and he felt their backs and haunches like a farmer judging a pig. The Graf never lacked venison, I guessed.

How extensive this game-farm was I did not discover, but there must have been other pens hidden from us by the tall hedges, containing less docile creatures than deer, for at one point, while we were stroking the noses of some fallow fawns, a curious whining broke out some little distance from us. The fawns took sudden fright and ran to cover: the keeper laughed shortly, but von Eichbrunn looked as unnerved as he had done when we passed the boarhounds and for an instant I thought he was going to flee like the fawns. It was a curious sound, and not a pleasant one: I have called it a whining but it was really more of a subdued and modulated screaming, with a babbling undertone and occasional shrill yowls of excitement and eagerness that sounded almost human; but it was wholly wild. It sounded like no hounds I have ever heard, and yet, I had the strongest impression of having heard it before and of having thought of hounds while I listened. Only some minutes after it had stopped did I remember where I had heard, or thought I had heard it before. It was exactly like the sounds my ear had seemed to catch mingled with the noises of the wind-stirred forest that night when I listened at my window to Hans von Hackelnberg's horn. I had fancied a whine of hounds then, and had reasoned that it must be the wind. But it was certainly neither hounds nor the wind.

I did not venture to ask a question before the keeper had led us out of his game-farm and set us upon a lane of the forest which the Doctor, evidently relieved to be alone with me again, followed at a rapid pace, uphill. Then to my asking if we were not going to look at the Hall, he grunted briefly, *"Nein,"* and explained no further until we came to the top of the hill.

He leaned against a pine tree and wiped his brow, for the day was very warm and he was unused to exercise. "No," he said, with some ill-humour. "I have had enough of the Schloss on an empty stomach. Franck, the gamekeeper, tells me that the Gauleiter's party are going to have their luncheon at the Kranichfels pavilion—that's a good hour's walk from here. It will be a damned good luncheon too. They are a paunchy, gorging lot by all accounts and I have every intention of getting my share before they come back from shooting. Then I am going to get out of this *verfluchte* heat and sleep."

"I thought you were going to show me the Schloss," I reminded him.

"*Ja,* no doubt you did," he replied; then, becoming less irritable as he cooled off, "if you promise not to run away this afternoon, perhaps I will sneak you into the Hall this evening. But I'm not answering for any consequences, mind!" he ended sharply.

I think I had taken the Doctor's measure by now; I thought him something of a child, so answered calmly that I supposed he would take care to avoid any unpleasant consequences to himself, and as for myself I was prepared to take the risk. On that understanding we carried on along our road.

He began to talk again after a while, in his usual

airy, conceited vein, but now I could not resist the temptation to deflate him by remarking that for all his superior contempt for mere sportsmen and hunt servants he must allow that they must have some skill—not to mention nerve—that he lacked if they handled dogs like the boar-hounds we had seen a while ago.

The effect surprised me. He seemed to swerve away from me, fetched a deep sigh and said something in German which sounded very like a curse on the day he ever took this job; then, very soberly he said: "The dogs are bad enough, but God defend me from the cats."

I was astonished at the real fear in his voice.

"Do you mean," I asked, "die things we heard squalling when we were looking at the deer?"

But he was offended with me for having made him admit his nervousness and he walked on in a glum silence.

Those few miles were full of interest to me. There was little life to see: no animals other than a red squirrel or two, and very few birds in this part of the forest, but I was most intent to mark the lie of the land, to memorise the way we took and impress on my mind each little side-path and noticeable tree or rock. We crossed a couple of little streams, from both of which the Doctor drank, and then climbed again, gently, up a long slope of ground to a ridge where the bushes grew very thick. There I suddenly heard the baying of a hound not far off. Von Eichbrunn seemed not to notice it, but a moment later started and swore as a man stepped quietly out of hiding in a brake and confronted us in the narrow way.

He was a green-clad forester carrying a light crossbow in his hand: a young boy, not at all ill-looking, who spoke briefly to von Eichbrunn and then watched him with amusement in his eyes as the Doctor grumbled ill-temperedly at what he heard. I half guessed what had happened, and had my guess confirmed as the Doctor, unwilling to be balked of his lunch, questioned the young forester again. We had arrived too late. They had begun to drive the game, it appeared, and if we continued along our road there was a risk of heading off the buck from the guns. The forester was evidently stationed there to turn back any game that might bolt away from the line of the drive down our path.

The hound bayed again; the forester cocked his head and listened; then a gun went off close to us, somewhere on our left hand. The forester still listened for a moment and then grinned. He raised his crossbow imagining a buck in range and shook his head regretfully. 'Had that fellow missed,' he seemed to say, 'I would have had him.'

Abruptly then, he turned to von Eichbrunn, and, as I gathered, asked him why he did not go to the butt near at hand and wait, since the drive would not last long. Von Eichbrunn shook his head, but the boy laughed and, inserting a finger into his mouth, produced so realistic an imitation of the pop of a champagne cork that the Doctor was immediately converted and allowed himself to be guided through the bushes without more ado.

It was by a kind of winding tunnel through tangled undergrowth that the young forester led us down the farther slope of the ridge. It was impossible to see more than a yard or two ahead, and the bushes on either side were so thick and interlaced that I could not imagine anything bigger than a polecat worming its way through them. It occurred to me that the place had been chosen and adapted specially for this reason, so that the driven game would be forced to follow known lines where the guns would be posted. When we came to the butt, I saw that this was so.

It was such a butt as no preserver of game in England would ever have contrived. A little copse, from the centre of which the undergrowth had been carefully cleared, leaving the saplings standing, was surrounded by a breast-high bank of earth well grassed over and topped by a fringe of low bushes. The front of the butt was a sort of demilune, having openings in its screen of bushes so disposed that from one or the other of them a gun might cover any part of the glade in front. It was, in fact, more a ride, or alley, than a glade, for the opposite side was a continuous thick hedge of bushes, looking natural enough to the eye, but no doubt layered and interlaced artificially in order to confine the game to the ride and force it to run straight past the butt within easy range. We were in a valley, and the ride, running lengthwise up it, ended where the ground sloped up more steeply and the sides of the valley, walled there with steep grey rocks, converged and appeared to meet or to leave only a very narrow pass between their crags. It was clear that any game being driven up the valley along this ride or others, if it escaped the guns posted oh them, must be stopped by the converging cliffs and either driven back again, past the guns, or shot by keepers stationed at the head of the valley. We had a clear view of a large part of that triangle formed by the cliffs, for the trees grew only thinly there. In the other direction, from which the game must come, the ride ran straight for perhaps a hundred yards, so that the guns would see the buck in ample time to be able to fire deliberately when it came in range.

It wanted only tame deer to make the worst shooter's success a certainty. And, having looked at the principal occupant of the butt I guessed that that was mainly the type of guest the Reich Master Forester had to cater to.

He was a short, grossly fat man in a pair of new *lederhosen*, with fancy braces, white stockings and an embroidered shirt. He was almost bald, square-headed and heavy-jowled; a thick roll of fat bulged over his shirt collar at the back of his neck and he had a stern on him like a canal barge. I could not have imagined a more absurd contrast to the three or four young foresters who occupied the butt with him: they so trim and fit-looking,

dressed richly in their greens and golds, but most
serviceably for the forest. The pale puffiness of his legs
and arms, contrasted with their sunburned hardness,
made him look like a different species of creature.

He turned his head as we came into the butt from
the back, giving us a blinking, uncomprehending glance
through rimless spectacles, then resumed his watch on
the glade again. He was seated before one of the gaps in
the bushes, on a folding stool whose seat disappeared
under the shining curves of his leather shorts, and
leaning against the turfed bank beside him were two or
three guns—one of them of the very large-bore pattern I
had seen in the Schloss. At the next loop-hole stood a
forester with a crossbow, keeping a careful eye both on
the glade and on the guest.

Von Eichbrunn and I retired to the back of the butt,
where he was greeted in whispers by the other foresters.
There, on a broad divan of turf, surrounded by
comforting flasks and capacious ice-containers, under a
tent of green leaves, the Doctor reclined at ease and I
had leisure to observe what was going on.

The guest had had some sport already, for a fallow-
buck, newly gralloched, hung from the bough of a birch
tree. He had evidently had more practise than game, for
I could see three or four empty cartridge cases lying on
the turf behind him. His companions were getting their
share, also; for at short intervals we heard the brief
baying of a hound and shots at varying distances from
us beyond the long thicket that bounded our view across
the valley.

Our own man seemed to be getting bored. He took
out a cigar case and was about to light up when the
forester in charge made a sign. The guest's loader
handed him his gun and respectfully turned him in the
right direction. The boy next to me nudged me and,
rising, showed me where I could look over the bank and
have a fair view down the glade. A couple of hounds were

giving tongue, hunting in our direction; then a red-deer stag came into sight, running easily up the valley. He stopped fifty yards from the butt, a little suspicious, but after snuffing and shaking his head, came on again at a trot, passing at a range of twenty yards from our earthwork. He had been driven neither hard nor far, and he looked quite tame to me—so trusting I would have instinctively lowered my gun had I been shooting. Our guest, however, blazed away. The stag had passed out of my line of vision then and I did not see the effect of the three or four shots our man fired, but, while the other youths leaped out of the butt, I saw the forester in charge retire behind a tree and furtively rewind his crossbow. He then gravely congratulated the guest, and while the boys brought in the stag, he stepped over to von Eichbrunn and chatted.

"*Das ist der Letzte,*" I heard him say. "*Jetzt haben wir nur noch the Voegel, dann wollen wir sehen ob's was zu essen gibt.*"

While some of them disemboweled and hung up the stag, two of the lads busied themselves with iced drink and sandwiches for the guest, who, weary of his exiguous shooting-stool, sank gratefully onto the cool, soft turf of the broad bench at the back of the butt. The lads flattered him outrageously, but, though he replied with a loud geniality and affected heartiness, it was plain that he had not particularly enjoyed his morning. He cheered up and began to show much more interest, however, when the head-boy, taking up and demonstrating to him the curious large-bore gun, began to explain the next part of the programme to him. I could not catch what was being said then, for I had moved aside, not wishing to attract the guest's notice, and was, in any case, more interested in some extraordinary new arrivals in our butt.

They had come quietly out of the bushes behind us and taken up a position on top of the earthwork, concealed by the bushy screen, yet able to watch the glade through the openings in the leaves. They were a young forester carrying a little whip and holding in leash two large creatures which, at first sight of their heads and fore-parts, I took for baboons. But when he allowed them to rise and stretch themselves, I saw that they were boys. Their heads were wholly encased in most life-like masks representing the dog-headed baboon you get in Abyssinia and those parts; the lips were writhed back in a realistic snarl, showing great, strong teeth. A mantle of silky grey hair mingled with golden brown covered their shoulders, backs and breasts and fell nearly to their waists; below that they were stark naked except for the narrow belt round their middles by which the keeper held them in leash. The exposed skin was very brown, but whether from the sun or by natural colouring, I could not guess.

The stout sportsman noticed them and gave a loud grunt of surprise. The keeper leapt down into the butt with them, and slipping them from the leash, set them capering about the space with a few flicks of his whip. They gambolled and postured on all fours and erect, imitating, to the guest's vast amusement, all the less delicate habits and gestures of their originals, and refining on some of the tricks with an ingenuity that put their membership of the human species beyond doubt. The guest guffawed and wobbled with joy, until at a word from the forester in charge, their keeper ordered them to come in, which they did at once, squatting and holding up their muzzles. He then handed them a fine strong net, which they swiftly took between them and threw over their shoulders like a rope.

This had scarcely been done when a bugle note sounded from down the valley. The keeper and his baboon-boys jumped up to their station on the earthwork again; the guest was led to his position at the front of the butt, and I slipped to the vacant loop-hole again to watch the glade.

All was very quiet for some time, then I heard dogs in the distance, more volume and a different note this time. Silence again for a space, then a shot, sounding somewhat faint.

One of the young foresters was standing beside me.

"*Da schiesst der Gauleiter los,*" he murmured.

I looked up, not knowing what birds they meant by Voegel but expecting something like black game or capercailzie. Another faint shot or two followed, and suddenly the dogs sounded much closer to us. They were driving up our ride, and now I recognised the voices of the boar-hounds, the savage brutes that had flown at the bars of their kennel in rage when we looked at them. I still had my eyes on the tree-tops and was listening for the rush of wings, when the forester nudged me and pointed down the glade.

A figure had come into sight, running hard over the shock grass: a human figure, but fantastically decked. It came on, running for dear life, and the unseen hounds clamoured close behind; there was no mistaking their intention to rend and kill now. The figure held my gaze; it was a tall, long-limbed girl, her head and features concealed by a brilliantly coloured beaked mask, which yet allowed her dark hair to stream out behind. To see her racing up the glade was as astounding as if you had seen one of the bird-headed goddesses of Old Egypt suddenly break from carven stillness into panic flight. A gorget of glossy gold and scarlet feathers covered her breasts; down her arms were fastened pinion feathers of chestnut and iridescent green, and from her waist behind swept out long, curving tail-feathers of brown and gold. These adornments and the yellow shoes she had on her feet were her only dress.

There was none of the tameness of the stag about her; she was terrified and she ran with a speed I could scarcely have bettered myself in the days when I was in training. I saw the desperation in the effort she was making as she tore past our butt and I knew she could not keep up that pace for another hundred yards. She passed beyond my line of vision and then I heard our sportsman fire.

Horrified, I was about to jump up on to the earthwork, but the forester, who had already raised himself so that he could see up the glade, exclaimed in a low voice, "Missed! Here comes the other!"

I looked back and saw another 'bird' running up, this one in white feathers, with a high golden crest and a short, up-cocked fan-tail. She was plumper than the first, not making so good a pace and beginning to show distress, but she made a spurt as the cruel clamour of the dogs swelled out anew behind her, and she swerved very near our butt.

I heaved myself up in the instant that the sportsman fired, and saw something that looked like a web of fine, brilliant yellow filaments—something like the tail of a comet—sweep through the air towards her. The girl bounded and screamed; the web seemed to open out, spreading as if it were carried forward by a great number of small projectiles about its rim, as a circular cast-net is spread, in the throwing, by the little lead weights at its edge. The 'bird' whirled about, slapping at her bare flesh as though stung, and, in doing so, entangled her arms in those fine filaments; she staggered and struggled, evidently smarting from the impact of the projectiles; ran on again a few yards, but with difficulty, for the filaments seemed to be viscous and, though so fine, exceedingly strong; they wrapped about her thighs and knees.

Our forester in charge now blew a cheery note on his little silver horn, and the young keeper slipped his baboon-boys. With loud, yelping cries they bounded down from the butt and raced towards the struggling girl. At the new terror she made the most desperate effort to run on and succeeded in breaking the trammelling threads about her legs, but the boys in a few yards were upon her. They threw her and whisked their net about her, subdued her struggles and rolled her tight and helpless in the meshes.

The guest was now helped out of the butt and the foresters prepared to pursue the first 'bird', whom we could see labouring up between the thinly growing trees towards the head of the valley, her reds and golds conspicuous against the cool green. The keeper called up his baboon-boys for the chase, and another handed the guest his gun, but our sportsman had had enough: he was not built to trot after such a runner, spent though she was. He examined his bag, squirming in the tight net, chuckled and snorted, ejaculated his *'fabelhafts!'* and *'Maerchenhafts!'* with tremendous gusto, but made it perfectly plain that all he was now interested in was luncheon. Von Eichbrunn was unhesitatingly of the same mind.

So the keeper and another forester went off to pursue the runner alone, cheering their baboon-boys on very merrily. A party of serfs was whistled up from the thickets to carry both the dead deer and the netted girl between them on poles, and we all trooped off to the Kranichfels pavilion.

My hopes of seeing the Count von Hackelnberg at the luncheon were disappointed. I did not even see the Gauleiter of Gascony and the rest of his party, for von Eichbrunn drew me away to eat with some of the under foresters in a quiet corner of the garden of the pavilion, while the great men made a very loud party of it inside. The young boys looked a little curiously at me and did not try to converse with me, but from their few quiet remarks I understood that the Count had left the conduct of the morning's shoot to his second in command. He had earlier shown his guests, none of whom had visited Hackelnberg before, his bison and his

elks, and had then left them to the amusement we had
seen in the valley. The Count, I divined, was too jealous
of his game, both animal and human, to enjoy seeing it
shot by outsiders. As for such attractions as the bird-
shooting, a plentiful supply of fine slave-girls from the
Slav lands and the Mediterranean gave the Count
material for many ingenious variations in venery with
which to entertain the Satraps of the Reich, but his
choicest game and his most curious inventions were
reserved for his private pleasure.

I asked von Eichbrunn what would be done with the
live game. He sniggered. "They'll be served up for dinner
tonight! *Ach*—alive and kicking, all right! That was a fine
plump pigeon our little man got. It will be a sight worth
seeing how he deals with her...."

The luncheon was extensive. The young foresters did
themselves very well, and our meal, I suspected, was but
a summary of the entertainment inside the pavilion. Von
Eichbrunn drank champagne until his English became
so slurred that I could no longer converse with him
reasonably and I resigned myself to losing the afternoon.
There was much I should have liked to do and see. I
should have liked to examine one of those filament-
throwing cartridges and one of the guns that fired them;
I should have liked to talk with the organisers of the
drive and to have gone over the ground; but neither
talking nor walking was possible.

The boys left us before the Gauleiter's party had
finished, but the Doctor lay in the shade another half-
hour until a lad came to say that a carriage was going
down to the Schloss empty and we could ride back in it
if we liked. Sleepy and obstinate from the wine, von
Eichbrunn insisted on our going back to the hospital to
enjoy a siesta, and I had no choice but to comply. There
he obliged me to give my parole that I would not go off
without him; so, while he turned in to snore off the
effects of his luncheon and the heat and the unwonted

exercise, I also lay down in my room and waited as patiently as I could until the evening.

It was after dark when he called to me, and he was in a bilious, peevish mood, so that I exerted myself to mollify and humour him, afraid lest he change his mind about going before we reached the Hall. However, much as he complained of his head and his insides, he seemed keen on the idea—anxious, in fact, lest through his oversleeping we might have missed the fun.

The high windows of the Hall were lit with an orange glow when we came out from the labyrinth of the Schloss and crossed the little park before the great building. People were moving about in the gloom in front of the high main doors, and von Eichbrunn led me with much circumspection round one end of the building, where, behind a buttress, we found a narrow doorway admitting us to a spiral staircase.

We climbed a short distance, then followed an extremely narrow passage faintly lit by a filtering of light through little slits from the Hall. This passage brought us to a small hexagonal chamber in one wall of which, about breast-high, was a round window, unglazed and barred, spokewise with delicate stonework. Obeying the Doctor's nudges, I peeped down through this and found that I had an excellent view of the interior of the great Hall, our window being situated in one of the angles, about thirty feet above the floor.

There was no electricity here, but the Hall was well and richly lit. Ten feet or so from the floor a stone cornice ran all round the walls, and on this, at short, regular intervals, stood more than forty figures which I took at first to be identical statues of silver, each holding a shining pole terminating in a cresset filled with steady yellow flames. When I looked more narrowly, however, I saw the figures breathe and stir slightly: they were girls whose bodies were either coated with a silver paint or cased in a skin of material so smooth and so exactly fitted that each living girl perfectly counterfeited a shining sculpted nude. The combined light of all their torches flooded the hall below and threw a mellow glow upwards to touch the salient carved work of the hammer-beam roof and bint at dark intricacies beyond.

On the two long sides of the Hall the cornice on which the torch-bearers stood formed the top of an entablature supported by a row of pilasters, and between each pair of pilasters was a shallow alcove. Along the whole length of the room before these alcoves ran a broad bench or dais of stone, thickly covered with pelts of bison, bear and deer, while in the alcoves themselves, on top of similar skins, were spread robes of soft furs- fox, otter and marten. Between these two daises, though a broad space distant from each other, stood the great Hall table that would have seated a hundred people with ample elbow-room for all. The Gauleiter and his friends were no more than a dozen; with them were dining some dozen or fourteen of the Count's officers. All sat, well spaced out, towards the head of the table, and at the head itself, facing our window, in a huge carved wooden chair, sat Hans von Hackelnberg.

I had expected a striking figure. I had imagined him, I suppose, as a man with something of the distinction of the old Eastern European aristocracy in his face and manner. The only correspondence between my image of von Hackelnberg and the reality was the wildness I had imagined. But the man who sat there, dominating the table, dominating the whole vast hall, had a wildness in his looks far beyond anything I had ever known or fancied. He belonged neither to my century nor the Doctor's; he was remoter from the gross, loudmouthed Nazi politicians round him than they from me. Their brutality was the brutality of an urban, mechanised herd-civilisation, the sordid cruelty of a loud-speaker and tommy-gun tyranny. Hans von Hackelnberg belonged to an age when violence and cruelty were more personal, when right of rule resided in a man's own bodily strength; such individual ferocity as his belonged to the time of the aurochs, to the wild bulls of that dark and ancient German forest which the City had never subdued.

He was a bigger man than any you have seen: a giant who made the great throne he sat on and the mighty oaken board before him look like things of normal size, and made the rest of the company appear like children at table.

His auburn hair was cropped short, which made the power of his immense skull and bull-like brow seem the more monstrous. He wore long moustaches and a forked tawny beard that glinted in the torchlight as he turned his head sullenly from side to side and glowered on his guests. The upper half of his body was clad in a sleeveless green jerkin crossed by a gold-embroidered sword-belt; a massive gold chain was round his neck, and on his upper arm, circling the prodigious muscles, he wore a golden torque of the ancient Celtic design.

He was not eating; but from time to time he snatched up the drinking-horn in front of him, drained it and returned it to its rest again with a fiercely controlled force, as if his arm, once raised, could scarcely be restrained from sweeping down of its own accord to strike and destroy; and now and again he slashed a gobbet of meat from the haunch of beef before him and flung it to the hounds crouching beyond the table, with a violent gesture and a savage glare that plainly said he wished it were the Gauleiter's head he hurled. Occasionally he tilted back his head and stared into the roof-beams, or let his gaze travel slowly and grimly along the ranks of torch-bearers on the walls as though ensuring by the menace of his brow that none dare droop or budge from her station. I saw then that his eyes were tawny brown and the yellow torchlight touched them once or twice with a red glow, like a coal.

We were late in arriving and the feast was nearly over—or at least, the guests' appetite for roast meat was sated. They seemed to have been served with rude enormous lavishness from great joints of beef, mutton and pork as well as game, and there was a true mediaeval disorder of greasy trenchers, vast pewter and silver dishes and plates encumbering the board. Young foresters richly dressed in satins and brocades went round filling wooden stoups with beer, and the big cowhorns at each guest's place with wine.

They were a rowdy company, already three parts drunk; they sprawled and bawled and roared out songs, one group against another with more noise and if anything less grasp of words and tune than twice their number of English undergraduates on a Bump-Supper night. Nor did they quieten much when six tall young foresters, most magnificently clad in green and gold, mounted a low platform behind the Count's throne, and raising up their silver key-bugles, began to blow a succession of tunefully varied hunting-calls. The Count threw himself back in his chair and listened to their music with a gloomy frown, and while they played, a troop of serfs hurried in and quickly cleared the wide table of everything except the drinking vessels.

When all was cleared away the buglers paused for a few minutes, then resumed with a quick, merry tune —some hunting song that was half-familiar to me, a galloping, rousing music which now hushed the boozy roarings of the guests and set them jigging to its own time.

The two wide double doors at the end of the hall were suddenly flung open and the slaves came in again at a trot, each four of them now carrying an enormous bright metal dish fitted with a domed cover. They passed down each side of the table, sliding their burdens on to the black polished board in such a way that each guest soon had before him a monstrous receptacle that might have held a whole sheep or stag. A party of slaves then leapt on the table and arranged themselves one behind each dish, grasping the handle of the cover. The young boys meanwhile went round, placing ready to each guest's hand a hunting knife.

Count Hans von Hackelnberg rose slowly to his feet; his officers sprang up and stepped back from the table, while the guests, more or less steadily, followed their host's example and stood, leaning and swaying and looking wonderingly from the Count to the dishes in front of them. The bugles blew one ringing peal and were silent.

"Gentlemen!" cried the Count in a voice like the bellow of a bull, "I invite you to partake of the game you have shot!"

The serfs in unison heaved up the dish-covers and swung them high above their heads, and then filed swiftly away down the middle of the table.

Exposed on the dish then in front of each guest was the 'bird' he had bagged at the end of the morning's drive, plucked of her feathers now, all but her beaked mask, and trussed tightly, knees to chin, wrists to ankles. The forester officers deftly moved away the chairs behind the guests, and with a gesture or two indicated where the 'bird's' bonds might be slit with the knife; then discreetly nodded towards the convenient alcoves behind.

The guests seemed to be too astonished to take these suggestions in for a moment; then the Gauleiter, on the Count's right, having before him a fine bronzed creature with the vividly ornamented mask of a wild turkey-cock glowing against the pale spread of her own abundant blond hair, broke into loud guffaws and leaned forward to pinch his 'bird's' rounded thigh.

Some of the others cheered lustily and flourished their knives, but before any of them could cut the cords of his fowl, Hans von Hackelnberg had hammered on the table with the pommel of his hanger.

"Gentlemen!" he bellowed again, and complete silence and stillness followed on his command.

"Gentlemen!" said the Count, in a more human tone, though still speaking loudly enough for us to hear every word in our little chamber, and with such deliberation and force that I could follow practically all he said: "I hope you may enjoy the carving of your birds as much as you did the shooting of them. The game is yours; let each man satisfy his appetite in the way he likes best, and if anybody finds the meat not tender enough for his liking, my young men will take some of the tough skin off for him." He pointed to his chief forester, who, grinning, picked up a dog-whip and drew the lash slowly through his fingers. "But," roared the Count, suddenly violently imperious again, "before you fall to, I invite you to come with me and see some of this same appetising flesh in a different hide. Restrain your appetites, gentlemen, for ten minutes, and I will show you a spectacle of womanhood which, I warrant, will put a keener edge on them. *Bitte! Herr Gauleiter!*"

He took the Gauleiter by the arm and marched him off to the main door of the hall, below the range of our view. The officers took the other guests in hand, and these, more bewildered by this sudden balking of their sport than they had been even by the unexpected offer of it, were shepherded in a puzzled and ineffectually enquiring flock from the hall, leaving their untasted delicacies to cool, as it were, on the plate under the eyes of the young forester-pages, who prepared to lounge out the interval which wine-cups in their hands on the skin-covered daises.

As the guests herded out of the hall the torch-bearers on the two long cornices turned left and right, and marched out through openings in the angles at the ends of their stone shelves, leaving only a third of their number still immobile on the end cornices to illuminate the hall.

The Doctor swore petulantly at finding the entertainment interrupted when it had scarcely begun. Then he plucked me urgently by the sleeve, whispering, "Let's go down and get a drink, at least, before they come back." And he promptly began to pull me along the narrow passage from our chamber.

I had no choice but to follow, but managed to enquire why we should not go and see the other spectacle. "No, no, no!" cried the Doctor with surprising vehemence. "I will not! For God's sake, let's get a drink!"

He tumbled down the spiral staircase, and I hard on his heels, but before we reached the outer air I had resolved to give him the slip. The yellow torches, formed into two regular lines, were moving with a steady pace through the dark some little distance from the hall; there was a considerable crowd of serfs and other indistinctly seen people standing about the end of the building, and as the Doctor scurried round to gain the main door, I had no difficulty in shaking off his hold on my sleeve and mingling with the silent crowd. I did not even hear him call after me as I shouldered my way through the serfs and hurried after the torches. I think he was too afraid of the darkness of the Schloss to stay out of the Hall by himself.

I caught the tail of the procession in a few minutes and attached myself to a knot of forester officers who were bringing up the rear. No one took any notice of me, though the light from the torches that flanked the party must have shown them my face and my plain costume. The silver-skinned girls, who looked as tall as grenadiers now that I was close beside them, marched with a deliberate ceremonial step, lifting their knees high at each pace, staring straight to their front and bearing their torches stiffly and steadily. The foresters conversed a little among themselves in low tones, but the guests, cooled by the night air, were strangely silent, and Count von Hackelnberg, still gripping the Gauleiter by the arm,

stalked ahead, towering over everyone, and offering not
a word of explanation.

We proceeded in this way for some hundreds of
yards, until, judging by the tall hedges we had passed, I
guessed that we had gone somewhere to one side of the
game-park I had seen that morning. The two files of
torch-bearers here began to wheel left and right, while
the Count and the rest of us stopped and watched them
until they had inclined again and formed a large oval
ahead of us. Then the Count, with the first note of
joviality I had heard from him, bade his guests be seated.

I edged forward and saw under the torchlight a broad
bank of turf rimming the lip of a curious oval pit. The
Count drew down the Gauleiter to sit beside him on the
inner edge of the bank, and the rest of the company
ranged themselves, with a little guidance by the
foresters, to left and right. I moved quietly off to one end
of the line and looked down. The girls now sloped their
long torches forward so that the cressets overhung the
pit and brightly illuminated it The sides were fifteen or
twenty feet high, revetted with smooth white boards, and
the floor of the pit was carpeted with closely cropped
turf. At each end was an iron grille closing a
subterranean passage, It was in miniature a Roman
circus, though plain and rustic.

A horn suddenly blew with a high, wild blast that
pierced and chilled me. I jerked my head involuntarily
round, as everyone else did—as even the torch-bearers
must have done, for a dipping wave of movement ran
round the ring of cressets. Count von Hackelnberg had
risen to his feet and had put his lips to a great, curling
silver horn whose shining circle passed over his shoulder
and round his body. He blew with all the power of his
lungs, and the loud, clamouring urgency of his blast, so
near, so wildly returned upon us by the close crowding
woods, was well-nigh unbearable.

As it died I heard the rattle of one of the grilles

opening. Out into the redly lit oval of turf came three young men, all clad from head to foot in suits of that strange armour I had seen in the keeper's room in the morning. I saw now it was not steel or other metal, but some material which, though obviously hard and tough, was flexible enough to allow them to move easily and lightly. The foremost two carried whips with long, heavy lashes of plaited leather, the third led two fallow does, two gentle, fat, dappled creatures, with silk ribbons round their necks.

They walked into the centre of the arena and stood there. The does trembled a little and pressed close to the keeper who held them by their ribbons; they turned their large ears apprehensively and lifted their heads with big, liquid, dark eyes that shone green for a second now and again as the torchlight filled them.

Von Hackelnberg blew another blast, short, high, peremptory, and before it had ceased I heard the response to it. That same savage caterwauling that I had heard in the morning, rising now to a shrill pitch of lust or hunger, came screaming nearer and nearer behind the second grille; there was the same horrible undertone of half-human babbling, but louder and more insistent now, the high, spiteful screeching which had so jangled the Doctor's nerves.

The grille was raised with a jerk and a clang, and there bounded into the pit some twenty large animals.

Cheetahs, I thought them for a second, springing forward with such eagerness they seemed to run upon their hind legs. But even before I clearly saw that they were not animals I heard great gusts of laughter from the Count and knew what he had intended by interrupting the lecherous pleasure of his flabby guests. The beautiful spotted coats shining sleek in the light below us were taut-stretched on the backs and full-rounded breasts of a troop of young women so matched in size and age and proportions that they must have been sought and selected with connoisseur's care among all the slave-breeding farms of the Greater Reich. They were strong and shapely, not fat, but in such perfect fullness of health and condition that the smooth curves of their limbs and bodies roused all the excitement that rare feminine beauty can, while the play of the muscles, flexing and flowing under the bright sun-tanned skin awoke in me something beyond admiration, an awe-no, ultimately a fear— of the power, the wild-beast power of sudden savage exertion, that those superficially lovely and womanly forms possessed. In repose they would have been models for a sculptor of ideal feminine beauty, but as they bounded into that arena, circling it with a fluid speed of movement almost too quick for the eye to follow, they were utterly unhuman: women transformed by a demonic skill in breeding and training into great, supple, swift and dangerous cats.

Their heads and necks were covered by a close-fitting helmet of spotted skin which bore the neat, rounded ears of a leopard, but the oval of the face was exposed, and each face as I saw it upturned to the lights was contorted in a grin, with red lips drawn back from strong white teeth, and in each pair of eyes a pale glitter of pure madness. Their screaming whimper now sounded like a lunatic song, and the babbling undercurrent seemed a crazy, tumultuous speech. I remembered the Doctor's remark about the dumb slaves and guessed that the surgeons had operated on these women too.

The tight skin jerkins covered their shoulders and arms and their bodies as far as the lower ribs; behind, they were shaped to a point terminating just above the buttocks, and from this swung a short-haired tail. Their feet and ankles were cased in a kind of high moccasins of the same spotted skin. But the feature of their costume that caught my eye at once and held it most was the queer gloves in which their tight sleeves ended. There was a shine of metal there, and hard as it was to keep my eye on the hands of any one of them as they raced and bounded about the pit, I could make out that each had fastened on her hands a pair of the strange, hook-like contraptions I had seen in the keeper's room. Imagine four curving strips of steel joined to some kind of flexible base-plate and one opposable strip fixed at the side, all arranged exactly in the pattern of a human hand, but each strip provided with a leopard-claw of steel with a hollow base to admit the last joint of each finger and thumb, and the whole thing worn inside the hand and fastened firmly with straps across the wrist, the back of the hand and each finger. I saw that the steel must be of spring temper, for they could half double their fists, and in their running they frequently went for a moment or two on all fours, touching the ground with their knuckles, and I distinctly heard then the slight click of the steel claws glancing together as one ran in that way beneath me.

As soon as the 'cats' had entered the pit the three foresters had come together in a knot in the middle; there, two of them, like a pair of ring-masters in a circus, facing outwards, kept the troop circling round, the length of their whip-lashes away from the centre, while the third held the two does, which plunged and struggled in an extreme of terror. The 'cats' were only half-trained, and it was as much as both keepers could do by constant exercise of their whips to keep them from breaking their sinuously flowing circuits and rushing into the centre. Each time one darted in, the heavy lash shot out, expertly cutting at her unprotected loins and rump, and at each crack and sound of the biting impact the screaming of all the rest rose wildly higher and higher, while she who felt the whip bounded high, dancing with pain and rage, shrieking and spitting and shaking her flashing steel claws in fury at the keepers. And above all that screaming I heard, gust upon gust, the tremendous laughter of Hans von Hackelnberg.

The keepers kept their cats racing round the walls of the pit until the sweat glistened on their thighs and their breasts heaved. Then the Count winded his horn once more, standing and blowing a long-drawn-out note with a dying close, the lamenting and receding music of the Mort.

As soon as he began to blow, the unbearable screaming in the pit below diminished to an eager whimpering, and as he finished the three keepers leapt aside and darted to the open grille.

Immediately and quite silently, more terrifying in their silent, swift intentness than in all their rage, the cats rushed in upon the two does. The poor animals sprang high into the air, but the bright steel claws swept and slashed, gripped and sank deep into neck and legs and ripped open belly and flanks. There was a moment of horrible, packed writhing of bodies, of vigorous thrusting of legs and haunches as heads and arms went down fiercely busy into the centres of two groups of cats; my nostrils were filled suddenly with the stench of warm entrails and I backed from the edge of the pit. A moment or two later the cats were scattered all about the turf, oblivious of their keepers now, tearing and gulping raw flesh gripped in their reddened talons. The only sound was the sucking and slobbering of their mouths or a low snarl as one brushed by another. Blood dabbled all their faces, the breasts and arms of their sleek coats and the clear bright brown of their bellies and smooth thighs.

Hans von Hackelnberg gave a hearty shout: "*Es ist zu Ende! Komm, meine Herren!*" The foresters jumped up, the torch-bearers turned and began to march off in two files back to the Hall again; the guests, in complete silence, shuffled with averted heads past the towering Count who stood waiting to bring up the rear, grinning and shaking with laughter, looking down on his deflated little flock of bullies with ferocious amusement. They had not the air of men going to enjoy the rest of a night's frolic I saw our own fat little sportsman of the morning, held up between two foresters, being miserably sick under a tree.

I lingered until the last pairs of torch-bearers were moving off from the bank of turf, hoping that von Hackelnberg would follow his guests, but some brilliant white lanterns were beginning to shine at the edge of the pit now, and fearing to be shown up, isolated and conspicuous, I attached myself to the last knot of four or five young foresters and marched past the Count with my head bent.

I thought I had passed him unnoticed, when a great hand on my shoulder stopped me as suddenly as if I had collided with the down-bending branch of an oak-tree. He wheeled me about, demanding to know who I was, and I found myself looking into that tawny forked beard, that wide, grinning mouth and those hot eyes from a distance of two feet. Abruptly, with his other hand he arrested the last torch-bearer, whose cresset swung above us and then shone steadily down on my face. The Count repeated his question in a voice of loud menace. The foresters closed in round us and, looking helplessly from side to side, I recognised one of the boys who had been in the butt with us that morning. Before I could collect enough German in my mind to begin to answer, he had explained. But I saw him tap his forehead as he talked, and the Count interrupted him, crying: "I know! I know!" Then, to me, gripping as though he would break the bones of my shoulder: "So! Thou art an escaper from prisons? Eh? Thy lust is to be free? So thou shalt be. Free of the forest! Drive him to the woods, boys! Turn him loose to find his fodder with the deer!"

He sent me staggering with a thrust of his arm, and the foresters at once seized me. I resisted them, instinctively, but they overpowered me. I had the sense to see the futility of exhausting myself in a struggle there and so controlled my temper and allowed them to lead me away.

7

They carried out the Count's instructions there and then. Though they had been, if not friendly, at least not openly hostile when I had been in the Doctor's company among them that morning, now they handled me with no more attention to my questions than if I had been an animal. They dealt with me with a brusque, callous efficiency, not actually striking me when I was slow to obey, but letting me see plainly and promptly enough how expert they were in dealing with any show of resistance.

They took me to some room in that collection of buildings near the game park, and there they made me strip off the clothes the Doctor had lent me and put on a strange costume which they took from a store that seemed well furnished with similar outfits. It consisted of a pair of knee-breeches made of some peculiar stuff, which might be taken at first sight for deerskin, but which I found to be a fabric, elastic as a living skin and with a nap on its face, short, thick and lying close like an animal's hair. They gave me a tight-fitting jersey of the same material with long sleeves, and then, taking a surprising amount of trouble over the job, fitted me with a pair of real deerskin moccasins which laced firmly and comfortably on my feet.

As soon as I was thus fitted out, they bundled me outside again into a yard where there stood a kind of small, horse-drawn van, or not so much a van as a square wooden cage on wheels. I was thrust inside, the door fastened on me, and with a couple of foresters sitting on top, I was driven off along a dark lane of the forest.

We went smartly, up hill and down dale over a fairly

good earth road for something like four or five miles, all through thick beech and oak woods. Then we stopped, and I was made to walk, the driver of the van going ahead with a lantern from his vehicle, the others marching on with a gun muzzle held in the small of my back. We followed a narrow, sandy path in an open glade. There was some cloud over the moon; I might by a sudden spring have broken away and given them the slip but that I was convinced they meant to do me no bodily harm immediately: strange as von Hackelnberg's orders were, they had been plain and obviously meant to be literally carried out. I knew now that the forest of Hackelnberg was most effectively fenced; to be free in it was only to be in a wider prison, but to be master of my own movements within those limits seemed to me to be a long step forward towards complete escape; I was not going to ruin my chances by risking a shot in the legs.

We stopped and the lantern shone on a tiny hut just within a grove of trees. It was made of a neat, close trellis of boughs and deeply thatched with reeds. They pushed me to the dark little doorway and one of them said harshly:

"Here you stay. You'll find food near-by. But if we see you we shall shoot you like a wild beast, or set the hounds on you!"

He lunged suddenly with the gun barrel and sent me flying forward into the dark hut, where I lay for a moment on the floor, winded and helpless from the blow. When I straightened up the lantern was already disappearing far down the glade.

I groped about in the hut and suddenly recoiled in fright as my hand touched a mass of hair that moved. I heard a gasping, suppressed shriek, and realised that the thing was more afraid than I was myself. There was a loud rustling of straw or dead leaves and something big blundered against my legs in a scrambling bolt for the doorway. I grabbed at it and found myself clutching a man.

He collapsed weakly on the ground, sobbing and muttering in so low and broken a voice that I could not tell whether he was uttering words or only those distorted sounds which were all that the Count's slaves could produce. Then, as I got my hands under his shoulders and lifted him up, he became calmer and I distinguished that he was speaking French.

He allowed me to pass my hands over his head and body, though he trembled and groaned a little in fear. His hair and beard were long, and he was wearing the same kind of skin-like garments as I was myself. He was a small man, and, I guessed, a good deal older than I. Doing my best to reassure him in my bad French, I drew him over to sit down beside me on a pile of dry straw which I felt at the back of the hut.

At length he was confident enough to begin timidly feeling my features and clothes in turn, and to ask me who I was. I answered him very briefly that I was an Englishman who had escaped from a prison camp, that in running away I had blundered into the fence of rays round Hackelnberg forest, and after being treated by the Doctor had now been turned loose in the forest by the orders of the Count von Hackelnberg. He shuddered at the name and groaned very deeply.

"They will kill you," he said, half weeping. "They will kill you. They will kill us all. They drive me from place to place. They drive me and there is no rest. I cannot sleep. I am going mad!" And he repeated the word 'mad' a dozen times, his voice rising to a shriek of terror and despair that appalled me.

I soon became convinced that he was in fact very near to madness, crazed by some abominable terror that I could not get him to describe explicitly. I thought to calm him more by asking him his history, but he could not keep his mind for more than a moment on anything but the horror that haunted and hunted him in the woods. He started like a wild animal at the slightest sound among the trees outside the hut; hushed me with a hissing intake of breath, and held himself rigidly clenched together to listen to faint, unidentifiable noises far away.

All I could gather was that he was an educated man —a writer, it would seem, for he babbled disjointedly, crying like a child explaining a misdemeanour for which it has been beaten, about some letters or articles he had written, jumbling together a collection of ill-pronounced German names and wailing: "I only followed *them*. I didn't know it was wrong. Why did they punish me? Why didn't they let me recant? They know I would never have written it if I'd known it was wrong. They misled me on purpose to have me tortured, on purpose to kill me to make them laugh. Oh, God! They're going to kill me for sport!"

I think half the night must have passed with my sitting there on the straw with that poor maniac, now trying to comfort him, now trying to elicit from him some clearer account of what it was he so feared—though God knows, I had seen my share of the horrors of Hackelnberg and could guess at others enough to send a man out of his mind. I could feel that the man, besides being under such mental strain, was mortally fatigued; but when I asked him what he did in the woods in the daytime, and where he found his food and whether this hut was his resting-place, he either did not answer, or muttered low with a kind of selfish, crazy cunning, that he would not tell me lest I betray him.

I was hungry enough, but there was nothing to eat in the hut; I was tired too, and feeling at last that I could help the man no more, nor he me, and believing that I had nothing to fear from him, I stretched myself on the straw and slept.

The sun woke me, and I found myself alone. Outside the forest was a wonder of fresh green and gold, cool, gay and delightful. I looked down the fair green glade, listened to the bird-song, stretched myself and breathed deep. My freedom might be only comparative, but it felt like real freedom; and in that broad early sunlight, with the sweet trees of the forest so real, so true to their own nature, so calmly and perfectly fulfilling the timeless cycles of universal nature, I could not believe that the evil perversions of natural beauty I had seen in the torchlight, the deformation and abasement of human beings I had witnessed the day before, were real. I looked about me for my little fellow-lodger, laughing to myself at his terrors, but I could not see him. I laughed at my own appearance: in those furry breeches I looked like a close-shorn Robinson Crusoe.

It amazed me that the Count's establishment should lavish such extremely good material on a criminal—as I must assume myself to be reckoned. It did not seem at all the Nazi way: they did not waste good clothes on human rubbish they intended to liquidate. But then I thought of the richness and elaborateness of the game-girls' costumes. Though I could not believe the little French writer's fears of violent death were justified, I had no doubt that he and I were destined for a part in some fantastic game of the Count's.

A little way off I could hear the faint murmur of running water. I pushed through the bushes and descended a wooded bank towards the sound. In a shady tract of beech wood, with little undergrowth, a small, clear stream came splashing over some rocks into an inviting basin of sand and pebbles. But before I could reach it, a savage burst of barking made me skip up the slope again and, peering from the bushes, I saw that there were two or three keepers with a couple of boar-hounds doing something at a rough rustic table a little way downstream from the pool. One of them was looking in my direction, and without any warning, he suddenly lifted his gun and fired. I ducked instinctively the instant

I saw the motion, and I heard the small shot go cutting through the twigs above my head. I ran crouching back towards the hut again, and did not venture down until I heard the snarling hounds being dragged off into the further woods. Then I went with great caution, warily listening and looking before I left the cover of the bushes.

I found that they had left on the rough table a good quantity of food—bread, cheese, potatoes, raw vegetables and apples. I was hungry, and was on the point of snatching up a loaf, when a sudden suspicion ran like a thrill of cold water over my body, and I darted back into cover again: it had come to me that I was being lured out to give the keepers a better target.

Nearly an hour, I suppose, I lurked in the bushes, famished, but afraid to venture near the table. They had succeeded by a mere threat in turning me into a wild creature. No, I would not confess that I was afraid either of their shot or their dogs, but the necessity to risk no injury that would wreck my chance of escape was overriding. The effect was the same; call it cowardice or caution, I lay with the patience of an animal, waiting until I was absolutely sure that the coast was clear. Then I ran down, drank hurriedly, and snatched up an armful of the provisions and retreated. I did not go back into the hut, but found an open, grassy space where I could look well about me while I ate.

That was the bitterness of my 'freedom'—knowing that I was turned loose for some cruel amusement of the Count's, but not knowing what form it would take, what sort of malice or trick to guard against. The forest was fairer than heaven in my eyes, but I had no delight in it; all my senses were stretched all the time for signs of the danger that might be stalking me.

Nevertheless, I had a purpose. I flattered myself that I was made of different stuff from that broken-nerved French writing-fellow. I don't claim to enjoy being shot at, but I have been in a few actions and had bigger stuff than buck-shot whistling past my ears. So, feeling a good deal better for the food, I set off on my first reconnaissance.

I found the forest not at all as wild and tangled as I had expected. There were plenty of signs that it was well tended; except for thickets here and there the undergrowth was cleared away, fallen trees were sawn up and stacked beside the rides, and the grass of the rides themselves was kept mown short. Apart from its seemingly great extent, Hackelnberg forest was just such a piece of woodland as you would expect to find on a country estate in England. It had that air of privacy, and exclusion, too.

During the whole morning I did not see a living thing except a few small birds and a squirrel or two. That, too, astonished me, until I reflected on the manner of shooting practised there. What von Hackelnberg's guests wanted was game without effort, not the uncertainties of driving or hunting wild deer. But I had heard the Count himself riding abroad at night and winding his horn in the forest. What game did he pursue there, under the moon? I knew the answer to that question now, I thought, and I measured with my eye the hours the sun had yet to travel down the sky.

It must have been about the middle of the afternoon when I came to the fence. I had skirted a broad, gently undulating heath fringed with pines, and I had been keeping in the cover of the trees, making towards a tract of woods that lay beyond the heath. I came to the tip of my belt of pines and found between me and the other trees a very broad zone of short grass, bending round in a long, gradual curve as far as I could see to right and left. There were at least two hundred yards with no cover that would hide anything bigger than a fox, but more important, and immediately attracting my attention, was a kind of high wooden sentry perch in the middle of the open zone some four or five hundred yards from me. The top of the tower was enclosed and I could not see whether it was occupied or not, but I was morally certain that binoculars and rifle-sights were covering that open ground.

The defence itself seemed ridiculously inadequate: a single row of slender steel pickets supporting three strands of thin wire which shone bright in the sunlight. I wormed my way on my belly as near as I dared, taking advantage of the heath that grew a little beyond the pines. It did not look like barbed-wire, even, and in the daylight I could see none of that strange radiance which I had seen, or thought I had seen, in the moonlight the night I came to Hackelnberg.

I crawled a few inches nearer, and at my movement a brace of black-game rose with a whirr from the heath a couple of yards in front of me. I watched them sail away, making for that other woodland beyond the fence. The cock flew high, but the hen, a little behind, was much lower; I could see that if she did not rise she would barely clear the top strand of wire, about ten feet from the ground. But she did rise a little: I saw she had seen the wire and was going clean over. Then suddenly she dropped, killed as cleanly as if she had been knocked down by a good shot with twelvebore. I heard the "plump!" of her body hitting the hard, bare ground at the foot of the fence. And yet I will swear she had never touched the wire; I am certain that she was two feet in front of it when she dropped; and then, if she had touched it—a big bird going at a fair rate—I should have seen it vibrate, for it was bright stuff, quite visible. I glanced quickly at the sentry-perch to see if there was any sign of the bird's having been observed there, but nothing stirred.

I moved off, exploring, to my left, keeping within the bushy fringe of the woods. I found some places where I could approach much nearer to the fence under cover, and from there I could see that for a distance of about two feet on each side of the bottom strand of wire the earth was completely bare for the whole length of the fence; here and there on this hard-baked, naked strip I noticed little bunches of fur and feathers: the remains of other birds and small animals that had tried to cross the fence.

A half-mile or so farther on I sighted another tall wooden sentry perch; it was a good enough guess that they would be situated at intervals all round the perimeter so that the whole line of the fence would be under observation. Had it not been so, I reasoned, I should clearly not have been alive to lie here and observe them this day from *inside* the fence. I lay there some time in concealment, reasoning on my observations and making my deductions about that fence. I thought I had evidence now of the effective range of the Bohlen Rays, which, I supposed, were carried and discharged by the strands of wire. If the effective radius of activity of each wire were two feet, then, obviously, the whole fence constituted a lethal obstacle four feet wide and twelve feet high. A tunnel was clearly the answer. That the rays were not conducted any appreciable distance by the earth itself seemed to me to be proved by the fact that the grass grew thick and healthy just outside the two-foot zone. But the nearest I had been to the fence so far was about forty yards. Should I have time to dig, by myself, and with such implements as I could fashion, a tunnel at least fifty yards long?

I began to work my way back towards the hut quite early. I had kept fair track of my direction, marking trees and scoring patches of bare earth with a stone as I came, and so, in spite of some blunders, I reached my clearing again before dark. I had been debating in my mind the possibilities of evading whatever unpleasantness the Count planned for me, and had considered acting on the hint the Frenchman had dropped—that is, changing my sleeping place. But then, some instinct—call it obstinacy

or pride—revolted against being driven like an animal,
running like a cat before a dog and providing them with
the very sport they wanted. If they were coming to
torment me, better to be found in my lair and fight it out
there. I wanted my freedom desperately, but I think I was
genuinely more afraid of becoming such a timid, crazy
wreck as that Frenchman than I was of an unequal fight.

So I returned, went boldly down to the table, seeing
and hearing no one, and ate heartily of the provisions
there and carried the remainder back to the hut. Then I
collected a number of long straight sticks and contrived
to fix them in the form of a rough lattice to block the
door, so that, though they would not stand assault, I
should at least be woken up by their cracking if someone
tried to get in. Finally, I laid the stoutest stick I could
find and a good heavy flint beside my bed and lay down.

It was an uneasy night. It spite of my long walk I
could not sleep. All the fears that my occupation during
the day had helped me to subdue raced freely now, and
the unceasing whispering, sighing, rustling and pattering
of the forest were a fine field for them. My imagination
interpreted even identifiable sounds, like the screeches
of owls, as the voices of those abominable creatures from
von Hackelnberg's kennels; I heard some small animal
pattering among the dry leaves in the grove and fancied
the baboon-boys circling round my hut.

Still, it was no fancy that brought me bolt upright
just before daylight, staring at the grey square of my
door and straining my ears to hear the sound repeated.
I had caught the unmistakable note of the Count's horn,
very far away, drawing out on just such a long note of
finality as a huntsman would blow to call off his hounds
at the end of the day. It had been a cloudless night; the
moon was in its second quarter; the rides of the forest
would have been light enough. The air of dawn crept
chilly through my trellised walls and I shivered.

As soon as the sun was up I did my best to throw off

that feeling of numb helplessness. My plans were scarcely formed as yet; I had only some general ideas which I dared not test against the facts as I so far knew them, for fear of total discouragement. I set myself, therefore, the limited task of procuring some sort of implement or weapon, and the best scheme I could devise for this was to see if I could not beg or steal one from the Doctor's household. I could not believe that the nurses who had tended me so well would be devoid of pity or so mechanically subservient and priggish as the Doctor boasted.

I waited in the cover of the bushes until the keepers had been with a fresh supply of food to the table; then, taking a small loaf and some apples and stuffing them inside my jersey as rations for the day, I set off to find my way to the hospital. It was a long and tiring business, and it had its alarms. For though I avoided every ride and path which might have led me direct to the Schloss, I several times heard parties moving near me: heard voices of keepers and tramp of horses, and once I had to lie still as a stone in the long grass at the top of a bank while a band passed slowly up a stream-bed below me—two bloodhounds held in leash, four of the baboon-boys with their nets scrambling along in front of their keepers, and a couple more foresters bringing up the rear, carrying those filament-throwing guns and looking sharply about them.

I caught a glimpse of some of the buildings of the Schloss through the trees some time after noon, and, guessing at my direction, worked slowly round through the woods. It was only by luck that I found the place, I suppose, but quite suddenly, when the afternoon light was mellow among the leaves I found myself looking down a little tunnel of a path at the white walls of the hospital and the narrow strip of turf and moss where I used to walk with the nurses.

Again, I had no cut-and-dried plan. I knew where the

kitchen was; my idea was to scout it from the trees and seize any chance that offered to slip in and make off with a chopper, a shovel, a big knife—or any handy-looking bit of hardware. If the slaves gave me no opportunity to slip in unobserved in the daylight, I intended to lurk under the trees until they had gone to bed and then try to break in.

As I crept round through the trees and peeped out on the side of the building where the nurses' dormitory was, I saw my Day Nurse sitting by herself on a wooden bench by the wall, reading a picture-paper. On the impulse of the moment, I stepped boldly out and said, "Hello, Day Nurse!"

She jumped up with a shuddering little scream and stopped her mouth with the back of her hand when she recognised me. She stared at me in horror, with eyes so shockingly full of mortal fear that had I appeared to her by moonlight draped in the earthy cerements of the grave I do not think I could have affected her more. She returned not a word—did not even hear what I was saying, I suspect, but just stood there, frozen with terror, the backs of her fingers pressed to her lips. I don't know whether I should have convinced her that I was alive, or that I meant her no harm: I had no chance. A step behind me made me wheel just in time to see one of the other nurses turn and flee round the corner of the building with a loud shriek. Foolishly I ran after her, thinking to catch her and stop her raising the alarm; but she had already raised it: three stout slaves came running down the verandah steps with brooms in their hands and began to swipe at me, gurgling rough snarls in their throats. I fought back, but several more slaves joined them, better armed with cudgels, and I suffered some severe blows on my head and arms and shoulders. Then a window was flung open and I saw out of the corner of my eye the Doctor himself, with a pallid face, look out and scream encouragement to the slaves. I shouted to him in English, but he only screamed back at me with a kind of panic violence. I fled then, shielding my head from the blows and dashing for the cover of the woods.

The slaves did not follow beyond the first trees, but I carried on for some little distance further before sitting down to rub my bruises and think the situation out.

I clearly stood no chance of breaking into the hospital this night. Not only would they secure all the windows now, but the slaves would be on the look-out, and I would not put it beyond the Doctor to warn some of the foresters that I was in the neighbourhood. Obviously, this livery I wore marked me as the Count's game and they were all terrified of harbouring or succouring me against his orders.

In what remained of the daylight I travelled back some way towards my hut, but as the night came down, finding a patch of tall, dry grass beside a thicket of bushes, I decided to stay there. It was a miserably cold night and it rained a little towards morning, but at least I did not hear the Count's horn.

Hunger, I suppose, drove me to find my way back to the hut next morning. I had turned over in my mind a plan for stealing into the Schloss itself, getting hold of some other clothes, somehow, to change for this damning livery of imitation deerskin, and obtaining some weapon or tool from the stores there. If I could only manage to steal a forester's costume I thought that in such a mazy place as the Schloss, with so great a number of people about, I might come and go a few times in the dusk without being discovered. But I had to have some more food: that project would have to wait until the next night.

It was fairly late in the morning when I got back to my hut, and I assumed that the keepers would already have been with a fresh supply of food to the table by the stream, and gone away again long since. Yet, as I crept through the bushes in the bank, my eye caught a movement down there in the subdued light of the wood. I parted the leaves to get a better look and saw that it was not the keepers, but a single girl, tensely poised, turning her head rapidly from side to side, ready to spring away at the slightest sound, but wolfing down the provisions with a famished eagerness.

The rags of her costume were still recognisable, and I was sure I knew that thick black hair and those long legs. I remembered the party I had seen with bloodhounds and baboon-boys the day before, and felt extraordinarily cheered that they could fail—that they had not yet caught the 'bird' whom our fat sportsman's first shot had missed. She had managed to tear open her beaked mask and had thrust back the front of it on to the top of her head where the beak rose now like a helmet spike; she had stripped the wing-feathers from her arms and torn away her gold and brown tail-plumes, though the narrow, feathered girdle to which they had been attached still remained. The feathers of her gorget were sadly bedraggled and she was smeared from feet to waist with dried mud as though she had waded through ponds and marshes.

I puzzled how to reveal myself to her without frightening her away, and concluded that the best thing was to show myself boldly some distance up the stream where she could see me plainly and assure herself I was not a forester before I came near her. I moved round behind the bushes, therefore, then stepped down carelessly to the stream bank.

She fled before I reached it, bounding away between the trees like a very doe. Without hurrying I walked down and stood by the table, picked up some bread and ate and looked carefully about. I could see no sign of her. Then, after a few moments I called out in English. I caught a movement then of the leaves thickly clothing some low-hanging boughs and knew that she was

watching me. I spoke again, in English, thinking that
even though she did not understand it, the sound of a
foreign language would convince her that I was a fellow-
prisoner or slave. But there was no response and no
movement. I looked steadily at the place where I had
seen the leaves move: it seemed to me that she must
have climbed up the drooping boughs of a great beech
and hidden in the thick foliage.

Then, without thinking of that atrocious gap of
history I had so strangely leapt, or indeed, having any
precise memory of where and when in my past I had seen
the gesture, I made the 'V' sign; you know, Churchill's
gesture, that the propagandists told us was current in
occupied Europe.

The leaves stirred again; an arm and shoulder
emerged and returned my sign. At that I walked over
until I stood by the ends of the boughs and began to say,
as best I could in German, that I had seen her escape the
shot during the drive, that I too was a prisoner of the
Count's.... A very firm voice speaking pure English
interrupted me:

"If you know a comparatively safe place let's go there
and talk. You go; I'll follow you."

Marvelling at the coolness and control of her voice,
and strangely stirred to find my own countrywoman
sharing the forest with me, I walked slowly back to the
hut; but instead of entering, I went on to the open place
where my first morning in the woods I had sat and ate.
There, on three sides the view was open for some
distance, and on the fourth was a dense thicket before
which was a low jungle of rank weeds that would provide
admirable cover for a quick escape. I carried on through
the weeds, not looking round, and when I stopped and
squatted down, I found the girl close behind me,
crouching low so that she was almost entirely hidden by
the herbage. She cowered close there, like a partridge,
only her head with its bizarre beaked helmet visible to

me. She had a comely face, lightly freckled, with intelligent grey eyes. She had brought an armful of the provisions with her and as we talked she ate, studying me all the while in an appraising way, with an expression neither frightened nor haggard as I would have expected, but wary and sometimes, as she told me her adventures, defiant.

My own tale sounded lame and incomplete, for I felt I could not attempt to explain—or rather describe—my incredible leap through time. I wanted her to have no doubts about my sanity. Therefore I told her simply that I had escaped from a prison camp, assuming that something like concentration-camps would be still a feature of the Reich. I could see that to her the imprisonment of an Englishman in Germany was a banal enough occurrence. But she wanted to question me about my camp, my offence, my comrades, then checked herself as if suddenly realising and respecting the reasons for my reticence. I had reflected enough now on my unthinking gesture to be astonished that the sign was still used after a hundred years of Nazi domination, and cautiously I enquired how she came to understand it.

"Why," she said, looking surprised, "it's the sign they used in the Old Resistance, isn't it? I'm not very good at underground things—I didn't have time to learn much before they got me, but I heard somebody give a talk in our Study Group at Exeter once, and he told us how the old Jerry-Potters used to give that sign to one another, in the Troubles, you know, after the Invasion of 'Forty-Five. It's supposed to stand for the nick in the back-sight of the old sort of rifle they used then, he said. I didn't know any Friends still used it, but I took a chance on your being a Friend when I saw it."

She looked very young when she explained about her 'study group' with such a serious air. She talked with sudden rushes of confidence and equally sudden baffling reticences or allusions to groups of letters-initials standing for underground patriotic organisations, I suppose. But I gathered that even after a century of authoritarian German rule, resistance was still alive in England, at any rate among young people, university students, such as herself. It seemed, however, to be no longer an armed resistance: rather, a matter of deliberate deviations on subtle points of doctrine and party theory —fine distinctions that had a burning significance for her, but which seemed as pedantic to me as the disputes of mediaeval theologians. Still, I reflected, deviations from religious orthodoxy in the middle ages had led from the study to the stake. My job had been to fight Nazism in a man-of-war, but it was just as much a battle when she and her like fought it by perverting a party slogan at a Student Rally. It must have needed more courage, for I and my comrades were free, trained fighting-men with a mighty nation behind us. And the risks were the same: not death only, but all the torture and indignity that a vicious absolutism might choose to inflict.

I asked how she came to Hackelnberg.

She shrugged: "Usual thing, I expect: carelessness and an informer. I was lucky, though, because they couldn't prove anything definite against me. So I was just sent for re-education to a Bund-leader School in East Prussia. That's the sort of place, you know, where they train the officers of the Youth Leagues. They send foreign recalcitrants there—Nordics, of course, I mean. The mental climate is supposed to purge their minds of error. Besides, the cadet officers need material to practise Leader-Art on—they like to get Aryan recalcitrants, especially girls."

"But how did you get into von Hackelnberg's hands?" I asked.

"I ran away from the School," she said calmly. "That was wrong, I know. The Friends' line is that if they get you in a re-education school you must stick it and learn all the tricks and be passed out as a sound Nazi so that you can do covert work when you come back. But it was hell. I couldn't stick it. So I ran away. Of course, they caught me. They class you as a malignant if you run away, and that means you're drafted for service in a Reich Institution and you're under the same discipline as Under-Race *Stuecke*. That's how I got here. And that's enough about me. The point is, what can we do about you? You're in a much tighter corner than I am."

I said we seemed to be pretty much in the same boat.

"Oh no!" she said, with a very youthful and downright practicality. "I'm a valuable property, you're just a Criminal—a liquidation-piece. I don't know just what the Master Forester does with the Criminals they give him, but I do know it's something slow and messy. How much have you seen here?"

I told her.

She nodded. "I haven't seen those cat-women, but I've heard about them. And heard them. They'll be doctored pieces, I expect." The casualness of her tone shocked me more than the thing she suggested. The surgical excision from a perfect human body of the element that lights it with a human soul was not a nightmare fancy to her but a commonplace practice.

"I've been here six months," she told me. "I'm a *Jagdstuck*—a game-girl, kept specially for these hunts. They pick out the good runners for that: there's a whole collection of us—Aryans as well as Under-Race. In between hunts it's not so bad. The forester boys aren't bad fellows in their way, until there's a shooting party. Then it's the dogs that terrify you; you know you ought not to run, but you can't control your fear when you hear the dogs behind you. And you know they'd let them get you if you didn't run, because you'd be no use for sport and they'd make an example of you to frighten the others. And even the best of the foresters go mad when they're hunting you. I've been hunted different ways. Sometimes they have guests who want more exercise than this Gauleiter's party. They take them shooting wild deer in the outer forest, and then for fun they have a mock deer hunt here. They turn you loose a day beforehand and then track you with hounds. You try to hide in the thickest places you can find, but when the hounds find you they send in those savage dogs and of course you break out and run for it. They shoot at you then with a sort of little dart that sticks fast in your flesh and has a long coloured thread attached to it, so that they know which man has shot you. They dress you like a deer for that in this tough skin sort of stuff and just leave you bare where the darts will stick without doing any permanent damage. The things sting like the devil, though, and you can't get them out without stopping; but then, as soon as they see you're hit they loose the retrievers—those ape-boys—to catch you and truss you up. But you have more chance at that game: they have to shoot you in the right place because the darts won't go through the deerskin stuff, and if it's not a fair hit they won't loose the apes. I've been hunted three times like that and got away twice."

"But they track you down afterwards?" I said, and I told her about the party I had seen out with bloodhounds and baboon-boys.

"Oh, yes," she said coolly. "They were after me most of yesterday, but I gave them the slip in the marshes. They'll get me in the end, of course, by watching the feeding places, but I shall have had a good long run."

"But aren't you afraid of what they'll do when they do catch you?"

"They won't do anything. True, they let the apes play with you a bit and that's loathsome. But they don't punish you for running—after all, that's what they want you to do. It's no sport for them if you give up."

"But if you *do* refuse to run?"

"Then the dogs eat you," she said with calm finality. "But once you've had one of those darts in you you'll do your best to dodge them the next time. They put something on them to make them smart more."

We crouched there in the long grass through most of that warm, sunny forenoon, and it was the strangest of wonders to me to listen to that pleasant young voice, speaking my own language, talking with such an odd mixture of naivete and experience, with such frank acceptance of fantastic circumstances. After a while I realised that she had fully made up her mind that I had been a member of an English resistance organisation: there was a kind of deference, almost respect, in her tone when she hinted at my 'work'—as though I had been a master in underground activities while she was just a beginner. She called me 'Friend' so often and with such an air of conscientiousness that I perceived that the word must be the consecrated form of address among members of the resistance movement, and I fell into using it to her and saw how that pleased her.

"But what are we to do about you?" she repeated.

"I'm going to escape," I said, with confidence.

"How?"

"Across the wire."

She shook her head very solemnly. "It can't be done. It's charged with Bohlen Rays, you know. One touch of that and you're done for. We've talked about that-some of the other Aryan malignants and I. There was a girl who'd been hunted once and was so afraid of being caught again that she said the next time they chased her she'd make straight for the fence and throw herself on it and kill herself. Well, she was turned out again as a deer one of the times that I was. She hid near the fence. They found her and she was hit as she dashed out. I saw it. She ran straight at the fence. But she wasn't killed— not outright, that is. I saw her fall and I heard her screaming from the burns. But what they do, you know, is to switch the rays off if something big goes into them. They can do that from the watch-towers. They picked this girl up and brought her in again. I expect she died from the burns. We never saw her again."

I told her my own experience of the rays. "But I don't intend to rush the fence," I explained. "My idea is a tunnel."

She looked blank, and so I discoursed on the art of moling as understood by prisoners of war. She listened attentively and saw the obvious flaws in my plan at once.

"It'll take too long," she pointed out. "Even with two of us working at it. They'll not leave you alone long enough."

"But there must be other criminals in the forest besides me," I argued. I told her about the Frenchman. He seemed to have been free a long time. He seemed to know where to hide.

She bent her head until her face was quite hidden by the grass. "I don't know," she said in a low, hesitating voice, "I don't know what happened to him. I heard the horn ..."

"Well," I said, "I'm going to have a shot at it. The thing is to get some tools. You know the ropes here better than I do. Where do they keep the spades?"

Then, when I showed so bold a purpose, she took up the idea with enthusiasm, and began excitedly planning how to get hold of some implement. She knew the place, she declared: the Kranichfels pavilion. The men who looked after the valley where the butts were kept tools there. She knew her way about there, for the game-girls were kept there when a drive was being prepared. I proposed to go there that night and see what I could lift.

"No, no!" she exclaimed. "I will do that! You'll be spotted at once in those things. I can slip in at dusk without them noticing. There are slave-girls there and I can pass for one of them. Help me only to get rid of this headpiece."

The different parts of a game-girl's costume were so sewn on that the wearer could not remove them herself—at least without scissors or a knife. I hunted about until I found two flints and cracked one to make a sharp edge, then sawed through the stitching that fastened the mask to her gorget. The fine, solid workmanship of her trappings amazed me now when I could examine them closely. "Ah! German thoroughness!" she exclaimed scornfully and pitched the beaked mask into the thicket. "It's beyond belief what pains they'll take to get every detail just right. These forester officers are monomaniacs, and the most inhuman thing about them is the way they fail completely to see that you are a human being: they'll fuss and fiddle about with you for hours to get you exactly dressed for your part in one of their shows, and yet you feel that they understand nothing at all about girls, or human beings of any sort."

She had a fine steel chain bearing a numbered tag round her neck. I turned it over; there was no name-just a group of letters and a number. My fingers were against the warm, soft skin of her neck, and while she spoke I was moved to mark the new hesitancy, the deeper resentment in her tone; she was so much a child still and she had been so brutally arrested at the very beginning of the road that should have led her into the ever widening country of love and understanding and free human relationships. The current of her life had been diverted into such queer, cramped, twisted channels. And yet she had preserved a marvellous sanity and unwarped spirit. I admired at every moment her courage and cool defiance, but what moved me most, what at once humbled me and gave me a new hope and purpose was, I think, her innocence and freshness in this world of distorted things. In this forest of Hackelnberg she was like one of the fair trees themselves that all the Master Forester's mad ingenuity could not force to grow false to its own nature.

You see, until then I knew that I had been forcing myself to limit my speculations only to the problem of getting across the fence; but all the time the thing I dare not think about had been weighing on my soul— that appalling slave-world, I mean, that I thought I should find outside the fence of Hackelnberg. Now I knew that there was still some truth, some courage and pride, some of the old glory of humanity left in the world. We must get out of Hackelnberg now; we would escape, I vowed, and find her Friends.

I turned that little tag over and over, while she held up her head, tilting back her chin, accepting with a kind of quiet, trusting wonder, the caress of my fingers on her throat.

"There's no name on it," I said, and I was vividly aware what feelings towards her she recognised in my voice.

"I'm called Christine North," she said. "But I always got just Kit at home."

Well, it was not long we had together: a day, from the forenoon until after moonrise; a long summer day. The longest of my life. I feel now that I have never known anyone so well as I knew Kit; I feel that if I began to tell the tale of every little thing that I noticed and delighted in that day I should never end though I spent the rest of my life unloading my memory. My mind's eyes are still so full of that intricate sunlit forest. I think I can recall exactly the bend of every grass-stem, the shape of every leaf, and tuft of pine-needles, every pattern of light and shade, every beetle and butterfly that my eye fell on that day; the scent of earth and grass and pines is in my nostrils now; the summery singing of the insects is in my ears. And there was about it some rare quality that belonged neither to her times nor to mine: something like the mellow magic that lights your recollection of a summer day in childhood—the glow and loveliness of the lost age when you lived and played protected, secure from all harm and trouble, free to give all your heart and soul to the rare, immediate wonders of the living earth.

We roamed Hackelnberg like two lovers who have newly found each other in an enchanted forest. To each of us our immediate past seemed as remote and unreal as if it had been an ugly sorcery whose spell the morning sunbeams had broken. Hans von Hackelnberg seemed an ogre in a fairy-tale: we only half-believed in him—only enough to make our adventure more exciting. And we laughed and planned our escape as if it were a game.

We suspended our belief in the existence of a morrow; we had such delight in the discovery of our own pleasure in each other, such wonder in the boundlessness of our new-found country, and the excitement of exploring all the domain of our new-opened hearts was so wild and sweet that we seemed to contain the whole of the significant real world in our two selves; we alone, wandering in the joyful summer forest, were all the world.

All day we saw not a soul, heard never a sound of human being or hound. Our unbroken privacy bred such a feeling of security in us that we went slowly, carelessly, arm in arm along the grassy rides, played in the clearings and laughed aloud. So we spent all the hours of daylight, talking, playing, strolling idly, but moving in our meanderings later in the afternoon towards Kranichfels. We lingered to gather wild blueberries in heathy dells that Kit knew, and stood there waist-deep in the bushes, eating the berries from the hollows of our hands, laughing to see the purple stains on each other's lips.

A little before sunset we came to an outcrop of limestone rocks overhanging a brook which filled a little basin at their foot. We climbed up there and sat on a ledge of fine turf from where, peering down through the leaves beyond, we could see a few yards of the narrow path leading down to Kranichfels pavilion, which Kit said was not more than half a mile away. It was a perfectly still evening with the sun departing from a sky of cloudless blue. The rocks glowed in the last rays and warmed us with the heat they had drunk from the broad sunshine all day.

"Ah," Kit said, after a long silence, "with all the power that they have, if they could have preserved so easeful and lovely a forest as this for love: for you and me and for all other lovers to wander in while youth lasts...."

We sat quietly there until there was dusk under the trees. Then Kit began to pluck with her nails at the seams of her feathered gorget. I found a sharp splinter of stone and sawed the stitches and freed her of the last of her trappings. Such slave-girls as might be idling about the lawns of Kranichfels in this summer evening's warm dusk would be unclad, Kit said; that was the distinguishing mark of an Under-Race slave: except when she was performing a part in some display her summer livery was her skin. In the failing light, should any forester notice Kit, his eye would catch the glint of her bright steel chain and he would take it for a slave collar. For her return, after the hour when the slaves were normally confined for the night, she would trust to the protection of the thick darkness under the trees.

She slipped down from the rocks and bathed in the little pool, washing all the earth-stains from her skin. I went with her a little way along the path until she would allow me to go no farther; then we parted and I returned slowly to the rocks that were to be our rendezvous.

Still in that strange mood of confidence that no evil thing could befall us, still believing that the savage sorcerer's spell was somehow broken by my finding Kit, I walked openly in the grassy space beyond the brook. The sense that we were only playing a game was so strong I could not feel alarm or anxiety for Kit; I was full of a trembling impatience for her to come back, but it was impatience to take her in my arms again and feel her lips again. The task we planned to do together seemed less serious than that.

The dusk thickened and still I prowled about, listening sharply for the low call we had agreed she should give to warn me. The night noises of the forest had begun: the soft whisperings, the distant cryings and near rustlings that were now growing familiar to me. I stepped quietly into the thin grove of birches beyond the open space and stood listening there; it was not cold among the trees, but there was a clinging coolness held like an invisible fabric between the faintly visible pale boles. I moved on a little, and in the brooding gloaming of the grove I began to feel that wild-deer wariness, that readiness to start and flee which I had felt before when I was alone, come back into my body.

In a patch of long grass, which, very dimly, I saw to be laid and trampled as if deer or cattle had lain there, I trod on something that was neither stick nor stone. Picking it up, I perceived, more by feel than sight, that it was a deer-skin mocassin like the ones on my own feet. It was cold and damp and my fingers told me that the sole was almost worn through. An old shoe, thrown away in the forest—yet it made my heart beat quick with fear. I wanted to flee away with all my speed from that patch of trampled grass, but I forced myself to hunt about there, groping and peering for what would put my guess beyond doubt. I found it: scattered rags of stuff that feeling and smelling told me were exactly the same material as that I wore myself—the hairy garb of one of von Hackelnberg's condemned criminals. But the hair on these torn pieces was matted close; the stuff had been soaked in something that had caked and dried hard. As I fingered them I heard again in memory that long note of the Count's horn sounding lonely and final in the dark of dawn. I dared search for no more proof: there was no need; I knew too well the feel of the stuff that had congealed on those remnants. I threw them down, wiped my fingers, dry though they were, on the cool grass and went blundering out of the birch grove into the open.

The moon, within a night of full, had risen above the tree-tops and was whitening our pile of rocks. Fearful of the light now as much as of the grove's darkness, I crouched in the shadow of the rock and washed my hands again and again in the brook, as if by washing them I could cleanse my mind of its dreadful picture of the Frenchman's death.

I could wait no longer for Kit to return, but went groping down the path under the thick summer canopy of leaves which the moonlight could not penetrate, with some idea of warning her, of begging her to run back to Kranichfels, to give herself up again to slavery, to endure anything for the sake of a strong wall between her body and the cruel fangs.

I made slow progress, for in the pitch dark of the wood I was afraid of losing the path, and I blundered continually into the trees; but at length I saw the moon again, and, winking through the leaves, a spark of yellow light which must be from a window of the pavilion. I hid close there, where I could watch a yard or two of moonlit path, and waited.

A long time passed, and though I listened in vain for Kit's footsteps, I slowly took courage from the fact that I heard nothing else. The moon was rising higher and higher, yet no voice but the forest's own spoke to her.

Then I heard a faint clink of steel not very far away down the path, A dead branch cracked and that brief little noise of metal on metal was repeated. I softly called Kit's name and saw a figure step into the patch of moonlight, stand stock-still for a second, then glide into the shadow. I slipped close to her, speaking softly to reassure her. I found her arm, and felt that she was clothed: the soft stuff my hands encountered felt like some thick fine wool, or velvety fur, as short and fine as moleskin. She was laughing softly with excitement and elation, but she would not speak until we reached our rocks again. There she leaned, panting, and put into my hands a small-bladed, sharp spade and a bill-hook.

"It's taken me a long time," she said. "I'd forgotten where the tool-shed was. I dared not move about much till it was dark, and then the buildings were locked up. But I knew where the *Ankleidezimmer* was even in the dark—that's where they rig us out in our costumes when we're to be hunted. I knew there were all sorts of things there. It was locked up, but they'd left a window open. I climbed in and got these clothes, and then I found a door into a store was open and I got the tools there—they're new! I couldn't find anything for you to wear, though."

She laughed again and was so gay and pleased with her success that though I had been about to tell her of what I had found and implore her to go back, my heart failed me. Only when she knelt to drink from the brook and the moonlight fell full on her, I saw that there was such maniacal consistency in every detail of the life Hans von Hackelnberg ordained of his slaves that there was no escaping the trammels of his one mad theme: the clothes were a single suit of overall tights, such as a dancer might wear for practise, fashioned to mould the contours of a human form, yet made of stuff woven with marvelous cunning to simulate an animal's skin. As Kit crouched there on all fours with her head bent low to the water and her face hidden, with the moonlight glinting on that strange, glossy dark coat which clothed her uniformly from head to toe, she looked like a lithe and sleek wild beast that had slipped out from the darkness of the woods to drink. For a second she seemed utterly strange to me, and with a shock of fright I felt the net of sorcery fall round us once again and saw von Hackelnberg's red lips laughing wickedly as he put a term to our brief holiday as human beings.

I seized her and jerked her to her feet, to a human

posture, and when I saw my roughness startled her, I could only mumble nervously that her costume seemed so strange.

"I suppose it does, to you," she said soberly. "I've seen it often enough. It's what the slaves wear in winter: it will keep out the bitterest wind and the snow and rain won't go through it."

"Let's get away from here," I said, and picking up the tools I led the way, behind the rocks, away from the open sward and the dark grove of birches beyond it.

It was still not too late to tell her, and I should have told her; I should have told her that my plan was no good, that it was unthinkable than von Hackelnberg would leave us in peace for the weeks that would be necessary to dig a tunnel. But I had fired her with enthusiasm for the plan; not by my words only, but by my very presence and my tenderness I had convinced her that escape was possible: practicable because it was so desired now; and she was so pleased and proud of the way she had carried out her part of it, I had not the heart to break the illusion.

We walked quickly along the moonlit rides, Kit talking rapidly in a low voice all the time, arguing in favour of this or that place that she remembered near the fence, but I was listening with only half my attention. I had to think of another plan, and I could not. Covertly I felt the sharp edge of the spade; the bill-hook was the better weapon, but the spade was heavier. I asked Kit to carry the bill.

We were making for a part of the forest which Kit said was as far from the Schloss as one could get; a wilder tract, less trodden than the rest, where the undergrowth and fallen trees were not cleared away. She had hidden there on a mock deer-hunt and had eluded the hounds and the retrievers for a week. She had learnt to find her way back there in the dark by coming down by night to feeding tables in the more frequented part of the forest. As she recollected, scrub and tall heath in that wild part grew quite close to the fence. That was the place for our tunnel; there we would work by night and hide by day, and to get us food she would improve on her stratagem at Kranichfels and penetrate to the slave-quarters of the Schloss itself. The way to defeat German thoroughness, Kit declared, was to do something boldly absurd: the German boys would never conceive that an Aryan would deliberately impersonate an Under-Race slave.

So, Kit running on with gay confidence and I racking my brains to think of some other expedient, we came at length to some high ground thinly wooded with oaks and deep with bracken and coarse grass. The night was very still and by no means cold. Kit blew out a long breath and loosened her suit at the throat. "Lord!" she exclaimed, "I'm boiled in this thing. I wish I'd..."

She broke off suddenly and seized my arm, and the moon showed me her eyes shining very wide. "Did you hear?" she whispered.

I had heard it. At last, the sound I had been listening for since I found those poor rags of the Frenchman's clothes. Distant, yet very clear in the stillness, the horn had sounded. It came to us across the moonlit woods, a gay and prancing note, a call that on an autumn morning would have set my blood dancing. We stood stock still, listening and listening after it had ceased, not daring to look at each other again. It rang out again, triumphant, exulting, stirring, and there mingled with it now the brief eager baying of hounds that have found their line.

I gripped Kit by the shoulders. "You must go back! You must go back! Go back to Kranichfels. Go and give yourself up. That is the Count hunting me. You'll be safe if you're not with me!"

I was fierce in my insistence, but she would not be persuaded.

"No! I won't leave you. I can show you where to hide. They won't do anything to me even if I'm with you. I know the sound of those dogs. They're not the savage ones. They're just the ones they use for tracking. They won't loose them. We can shake them off. Come on! Oh, come on!"

There seemed a chance that what she said was true. In any case, our best hope of safety seemed to lie in reaching those thickets that she knew. We fled then, running steadily along a path through the thin oak woods.

I soon had proof that my past was not hallucination, for it betrayed me in this unbelievable present. I should have been able to keep up a controlled cross-country pace without distress, but I found again, as on my walk from Oflag XXIX Z, that two years of captivity, underfeeding and lack of exercise had robbed me of my strength and endurance. I began to stream with sweat in the first mile; I laboured for breath and my legs were like splints of wood. I tried no more to persuade Kit to part from me, not only because I could not spare the breath, but the hard fact was that I should never have made the speed I did without her. And yet it was bitter to think that even in fleeing from him we were doing von Hackelnberg's will. He had had Kit trained for just such work as this; I had a mental image of him admiring her long stride and easy breathing and grinning with malicious pride in his handiwork.

It was some time before we heard the horn again, and then it was fainter. We had gained on the hounds. But we had come into rougher country now and were scrambling down paths that were more like the beds of little torrents—places where one might easily fall and sprain or break an ankle. But my deer-hide mocassins and Kit's supple shoes gave us sure footing on the smooth stones, and with that fear behind us we took bold leaps downwards. I had a notion that the scent would not lie so well on the cold stones, so where we could we slithered down the wide slabs of rock that strewed the valley side. Our surest ally was water, and that, I saw, was Kit's intention. We plunged into tall grass and thin growth of birches and poplars at the bottom of the slope, and then I felt the ground yield and squelch beneath me. Soon we were in a weedy morass, wading deeper and deeper until the water rose to my breast. There we found a moderately firm bottom and, oaring with our arms, we went the length of a narrow pond that filled the middle of the marsh. We continued until we found the inlet stream, then followed that, stumbling and splashing among its stones and holes, climbing gradually up its course between the valley sides. It brought us out upon an upland bog and there we rested, sitting on the quaking turf.

"They'll lose time in the marsh," Kit gasped. "They'll have to circle it all to pick up the scent again. Come on!"

But she had lost her direction now, and we ourselves lost time floundering across that boggy plain, stopping, trying to recognise the shape of the low wooded hills about us in the moonlight. As we reached the firm ground again and Kit declared she recognised the place, we heard the hounds give tongue again.

We toiled on, running a little where we could, but most of the time going at a shambling, stumbling walk. Kit was spent now. We had no energy for speech, but went dumbly on, close together but each isolated by our own body's distress, by the imperious need to concern ourselves with our own thumping heart and labouring lungs and aching limbs. I still held on to my spade, hampering though it was, but Kit had dropped the billhook. I was too exhausted to say anything about it.

There was no path now. We were struggling blindly through tangled undergrowth so thick that in places it forced us to go on our hands and knees. I do not know how long we spent fighting our way through that scrub;

I do not know what distance we had covered in our flight; the stages of it were confused and jumbled in my mind; our present toil seemed to have continued for an age, and our wading through the long pond was something we had done long ago when we were strong and fresh.

I blundered into Kit. She was lying still upon the earth and she groaned at my touch. "I can't go on," she whispered. I lay down beside her, too spent myself to urge her on, and listened. Beyond our own panting I could hear nothing. We lay until we began to get our breath a little more easily, and still the silence was unbroken.

We lay there, exactly as that mad hunter would have us: turned by the terror of his horn and hounds into frightened animals cowering, pitifully hopeful of escape, in the heart of the thicket. We could do no more than hope that the hounds would fail; we could run no more. I felt the edge of my spade again and gripped the shaft. I would at least settle the business of a hound or two before they tore my throat out. But this was no place to stand at bay; I must have room to swing. Here the interlaced boughs of the scrub held me fast; a hound could come worming on its belly to seize me like a ferret fastening to a rat in a hole. I tried to move Kit to crawl on to some more open place.

"This is the thickest part," she said wearily. "The fence can't be far away. Our best chance is to lie still here. It's only more sport for them if they get you in the open."

I lay till I had recovered my strength somewhat, but then the inaction, the waiting in that silence, was too much for me. Dragging my spade along I began to creep forward to find how far our thicket extended.

I called softly back once or twice as I went and heard Kit answer. I did not intend to go out of range of her voice lest we lose one another. The scrub grew a little thinner after some distance and I found I could go erect, pushing through with my shoulders, though I could still see nothing about me, only glimpses of the moon above. I did not think I had gone very far from Kit when I pushed right out of the bushes into open heath. I dropped down at once into the low cover, for there was a watch-tower three or four hundred yards away from me on my flank. In front, only fifty or sixty yards across the heath, I could see the fence: a wall of faint radiance as I had seen it that other moonlight night, though I thought now that I could distinguish the paler lines of the wires running through it. I crawled along the edge of the scrub to my left away from the watch-tower, keeping, as I thought, at about the same radius from the place where I had left Kit.

I found the scrub inclining gradually away from the fence as I went and suddenly I had a clear view down a long open space, a kind of broad, though much neglected, ride that cut straight through this tract of wild forest. It might have been an old fire lane, and it led straight up to the fence. Realising that had we been a hundred yards or so to our left we could have reached our present hiding-place without all that long toil through the scrub, and realising also, with a sinking heart, that on two sides we were very near the edge of our cover, I sat down to think out what was best to do. I had scarcely settled myself in the tall herbage when I heard the baying of the hounds somewhere behind me.

They were terribly near now, and I knew that full, sure note of their voices well. I strained my ears and caught another sound—the cracking of dry twigs under human feet. A long, cheerful "Halloo!" sounded clearly from the scrub and was taken up by someone more distant down the ride. I dare not risk a call to Kit, but began to crawl into the bushes again to try to rejoin her. Then I stopped, reflected and went back into the ride and crouched in the withered weeds again. The hounds were laid on my line—of that I was certain, for they did not hunt game-girls by night. Kit also knew that. Surely, then, I reasoned, she would think of crawling away from our line; the bloodhounds would not change quarry when my scent was so hot: they would pass her in the scrub, follow my scent out and circle round to find me in the open. I took a good grip on my spade and waited.

I heard them baying again, and now they seemed to me to have surely passed the place where I had left Kit. I half rose, changing my plans, thinking now that I had got my wind again I could run down the ride and draw them clear away from her. But before I could straighten up there came a loud, ringing clamour of sound from down the ride: the high, exulting pealing of the Count's horn, imperiously rousing and commanding, the thudding beat of horses' hooves and, terrifyingly near and shrill, appalling in its unexpectedness, that torrent of mad screaming and babbling distortion of human utterance that I had heard twice before in Hackelnberg.

Hans von Hackelnberg was riding up the long glade with all his cats screeching for blood. They came nearer with dreadful speed and in my horror I could neither stand nor flee. I saw dark shapes of horsemen cantering up through the long grass and heath, and saw in front of them a dozen—no, a score and more—of human shapes, but shapes that bounded rather than ran, covering the rough tangle of herbage with long, flying leaps. I saw those panther heads shoot up in black silhouette against the moonlit sky; I saw the shapes bend, tawny-grey against the grass, and saw again their leaping limbs flash pale in the milky light. The hounds bayed behind me, hunting somewhere close to the fence where I had been, but I paid them no attention now. I could only watch those shapes bounding on towards me; could think of nothing but the glint of steel at the end of their dark arms. Then I saw ride forward among them a man who looked gigantic in the moonlight: one who wore round his breast a gleaming coil of silver. He blew

another blast, loudly and insolently proclaiming the right
to slaughter for lust. I wiped my palms on the hair of my
breeches and slowly rose and backed against a thick
bush and swung my weapon.

There was a sudden loud shout from someone
behind Hans von Hackelnberg; the Count himself reined
in his horse and blew one sharp call on his horn. The
screaming and babbling of the cats concentrated all at
once in a sustained screech. But it was not I that they
had seen.

A dark form had slipped out of the scrub and was
crossing the moonlit open a few yards in front of the
pack. It turned and fled straight up the ride towards the
fence.

The cats flew forward over the heath and tussocks.
Their screeching ceased, but as they hurtled past me I
heard one loud sob as if it were one common intake of
breath, or as if every fierce mouth had suddenly drunk
in at once a draught of air already heavy with the odour
of their victim's blood. The black figure still led them,
running as a human being runs for life, but straight
towards that wall of pale radiance, that whiter light
within the blue-white of the moonlight. Too late, I saw
that she would not swerve. Without knowing what I was
going to do, without caring for Hans von Hackelnberg or
his cats or his hounds, I cried out and began to run after
her.

Von Hackelnberg had seen Kit's purpose, too. He
thundered after his pack, cursing at the top of his great
voice, then began to blow wild short blasts, calling the
cats off. His followers galloped after him; I heard long,
loud whistles shrilling above the Count's horn.

But the cats had their quarry clear in sight; they
were gaining on her fast and I knew nothing could call
them back now. I saw Kit leap at that insubstantial
luminous barrier as if it had been a solid wall that she
could scale, and I shouted out her name, cold with

horror to see her, who had seemed by her sanity to prove my own, driven mad by fear. But in the next moment I knew it was not so. Even as she sprang at the fence she called to me. I heard her, above all the shouting and the whistling and the blowing of the horn, I heard her calling, not madly but with a terrible devotion: "Alan! Alan! Cross, cross; oh, cross!"

Then below her, against that screen of faint white light, the pack piled in a mass of twisting bodies and wildly upflung arms, all black against the radiance. And now I heard them cry again—short, frantic shrieks and moans of agony. The shadowy shapes of the horsemen plunged and danced on this side, between the fence and the scrub; the whistles blew continuously and von Hackelnberg's horn rang out, peal upon peal.

I kept on towards them, running up through the thin bushes on the edge of the thicket, and all the time my eyes were fixed on that black figure above the writhing body of the pack; for it hung there, very still, both arms straight stretched out as though lying along the topmost wire, her head fallen forward and her legs hanging limply down. She hung there, dead in the very sign of sacrifice and salvation. And as I halted, knee-deep in the rough grass and ling that ran away to the fence, I saw Kit's figure shine with a dim incandescence as if each fine hair of the velvet pelt that sheathed her were touched with hoar-frost.

My brain and heart both were so bruised by that blow that I forgot the danger she had tried to draw from me. I think I had begun to stumble across the open towards her, crying her name, when, as real as an actual echo, her voice sounded again in my ear: "Alan! Cross!" And then I saw why she had rushed on death and I remembered how she herself had seen the thing happen once before. The radiance of the fence faded swiftly away and the whistles stopped shrilling. I caught a glimpse of the wire glinting cold in the moon and had a second's impression of heather and birches beyond it and a black mass of pine forest farther away before a searchlight beam shot down from the watch-tower. It fingered the fence for a moment, then found the group by the wire and held it.

I saw then quite coolly what I must do. The foresters had ridden in close to the fence. I heard the slashing of their heavy whips and sharp howls of pain cutting the demented screaming and the moaning. The tangle of bodies and limbs rolled back, away from the fence, and broke up into a dozen cats who scattered among the horsemen, snarling, spitting, screeching, flying back to claw and tear at their injured mates, while their keepers hewed and swore, flogging them off and herding them away to the edge of the scrub again. I ran forward under the searchlight beam, sure that all who were held in it were blind to me, sure that the dog-boys were holding in their bloodhounds believing their work to be finished and sure that the sentries in the tower had all their attention fixed on the wreck of the pack. I crossed those two yards of bare earth at the fence, felt the wire with my hand, slipped through and ran crouching through the heather on the other side towards Kit's body.

Before I reached it Hans von Hackelnberg and a couple of his foresters had sprung down from their horses. They strode among the forms that lay upon the earth, some still, some squirming, and with short, violent thrusts of their falchions the two boys quietened each cat that still moved. Hans von Hackelnberg marched straight to that body hanging on the fence. He plucked it from the wire and swung it above his head in his huge hands. I had been invisible to him for I was outside the dazzling beam, but now I started forward and he saw me in the penumbra, not twelve feet from him, with the slight fence between.

The boys too saw me and advanced their blades as though to charge on me, but von Hackelnberg halted them with a short bellow. He stood there, holding the limp body with all its shroud of ashy velvet shimmering in the beam, then slowly turned and looked towards the whimpering remnant of the pack which the mounted foresters could scarcely keep at bay. He checked himself and half turned towards me again. The brilliant light made of his features a caricature of rage and cruelty more inhuman even than the creatures of his own evil ingenuity, but I was not afraid of him any more. I looked from his ferocious strength to the pitiful dead thing he held, and learned then for the first time how such a loss uproots all other agonies from the soul and makes of the heart a desert where fear and pain can never grow again. I was indifferent to his violent shout at me and did not understand it until long after he had turned away.

"Go!" he howled at me. "Go free this night. Hans von Hackelnberg spares thee now to hunt thee again under another moon!"

I did not know or care by what law of his own mad sport he spared me. The foresters fell back and sheathed their falchions. I should have crossed the fence again then and gone to meet the steel-clawed brutes, but the searchlight beam slid back into its tower, the white rays of the fence made one long leap back across all the open, and I saw von Hackelnberg with his burden through that strange screen, colourless, shadowless, robbed of all substance, remote from me as I from the white, tranquil moon. I saw his blank and ghostly form stride on towards the phantom pack, heave the pale body high again and hurl it among them.

I do not know how long I lay on the heath, staring into that thin, luminous wall. I must have gazed into it until long, long after any shape had ceased to stir beyond it, unable to think or move. I heard nothing, I saw nothing more. There is no record in my brain of what ensued later that night—or many nights after; only my body still has a kind of physical memory that I rose and tore von Hackelnberg's livery off it, and that I walked in a trance of weariness through the woods, walked on and on until moonlight and shadow swung together before my eyes, until I was stone-blind and the earth fled from beneath me.

8

The cat, which had been sleeping quietly on the hearthrug for the last hour of Alan Querdilion's story, woke as he ceased speaking, yawned and jumped on to the arm of his chair. He rose, kicked the end of the last log into the nearly dead fire and shivered with cold.

"The German police had not much doubt that I was barmy," he said, "when they found me like that, wandering stark naked by the railway line. It was at a little place called Kramersdorf, not far, it seems, from Daemmerstadt—the station I had been making for. They kept me in hospital for a month and then, either because they thought I was cured or because they didn't much care anyway, they put me back in the cage: a different camp, though. That was in September, nineteen-forty-three. I stayed there till the Russians came in May, forty-five."

"But have you no idea where you'd been? ..." I began. "I mean, did the German police not trace what you'd been doing between escaping from your first camp and being picked up on the railway line?"

"If they did they never told me," he said.

He was silent a long time, and then sighed.

"Ah, well, that's all that happened to me while I was round the bend. As I told you, if it doesn't happen again for another year I shall ask Elizabeth to marry me, and I hope I shall forget I was ever mad. You've kept awake through the tale, now you must go to bed and forget you ever heard it. No one else ever will."

"No," I said. "Elizabeth must hear it. You must tell it to her."

He went out without replying, and I heard him unfastening the front-door bolts.

"I don't know," he muttered, as if to himself. "I don't know." He swore suddenly under his breath. "Where's Smut gone to again? Cats are a damn nuisance, whether you let them out or try to keep them in."

Milton Keynes UK
Ingram Content Group UK Ltd.
UKHW012046310124
437050UK00006B/572